The CURSED SPIRIT 2

A TALE OF CHARLES ISLAND

MARISSA D'ANGELO

Dedication

This book is dedicated to my Grandpa Haborak. You were a creative man and always strived for the best. I always knew that you never stopped loving Grandma, no matter what.

Books by Marissa D'Angelo

Tales of Charles Island Series

The Cursed Spirit

The Cursed Spirit 2

The Cursed Vessel

The Cursed Inn

The Cursed Monastery

Presence

Other Books

The Vanished

Chasing Time

Author's Note

Since the release of this book, I have wanted to find some way to help Charles Island and the wildlife that it supports. A local reforestation group is working hand in hand with the Connecticut Department of Energy and Environmental Protection to plant more trees so that the island and its wildlife can survive and thrive.

Message from Reforestation Group:

We want to restore the island to its former state. After years of invasive species and diseases, we need to help nature along with this task.

<u>10% of the proceeds from this series will go towards the Paugussett Tribe & reforestation group</u>

Aponi

1

Desolate trees towered over the forest floor; bare of any leaves. Streams of sunlight glistened through their barren branches; robbed of the vibrancy they once were full of. Contrasted with the sullen trees was the darkened soil that laid beneath. What were once bright green stalks of grass were now blanketed by leaves of various colors. The vibrant and lively summer colors had withered into shades of yellow, brown, and orange. Creeping by each towering tree, I couldn't help but connect with the sight that surrounded me. I, too, felt I had once been full of vibrancy and life as the trees did in spring and summer. But now…just like them, whatever remained within me that even resembled the slightest bit of life now diminished and wilted. At times, I felt I had nothing more to give, but as I traced my fingers against the bark, I couldn't help but feel a glimmer of hope. Even after they lost all that made them live, they somehow found a way to continue on. In fact, they didn't need their old leaves and instead, grew new ones that would allow them to thrive again. We all have something to learn from nature and this is the very thing that helped me to continue on after all the turmoil. Dawn had just broken and the fiery sun arose from its long rest at night. The remaining birds that hadn't left for a warmer place continued to call out their songs, never letting go of their tradition of rising with the sun. Spring would breed an entire forest of birds who nested in these same trees. Seeing the emptiness that would someday turn into much more gave me hope. With each step, the brittle leaves unavoidably crumbled. I winced at the noise I made, since any animal I hunted would likely hear me coming. It was not easy to creep around them since everywhere you looked were more and more piles of leaves. For a brief moment, I paused and attempted to stay as quiet as I could. While I listened intently to my surroundings, it was difficult to block out the continuous melodies from birds that, for some strange reason, stayed up here when it became cold. I squeezed my eyes shut. The only thing I needed to do right now was listen. Coming from what sounded like just a few steps away was a repetitive scampering that I wouldn't have been able to hear if not for the leaves that broke upon each movement. Another animal had been rummaging through the forest floor and now I knew the noise did not just come from my own footsteps.

If I moved too quickly, the prey I had been hunting would be long gone. My eyes had still been closed while I focused entirely on what I heard. Slowly opening each eye, I turned in the direction the sound came from and crouched down. Unable to press my knees to the ground, I gently took steps closer while remaining low. Everything before me seemed to blend into one another. Dark, warm bark from the trees led right into even more of the same shades. Standing out from the dry, brittle leaves was a much smoother patch of fur. Slight movements revealed a small rabbit that matched almost too perfectly with its surroundings. If it weren't for its sudden turns, I wouldn't have been able to find it as easily. It hopped a few spaces over, looking out in the distance...it almost appeared to be staring in the exact direction of the path to the island. Carefully reaching behind my back, I pulled an arrow from the bag that was draped over my shoulder. After I rested it on the bow, I pulled back and aimed directly at the rabbit. As soon as I was ready to release my arrow, which would send it gliding into the meal that could assist in the tribe's survival of the upcoming winter, the rabbit turned to look straight at me. Its slender body proved that it, too, hungered for any kind of sustenance in preparation for the cold that would inevitably come. With mere luck, I ended up on the side of having the small rabbit's life in my hands. In the matter of seconds,

I could choose its fate. It carefully lifted its paw and darted away in a flash. The moment's hesitation on my part allowed the rabbit ample time to scurry away in that same direction it had been looking before…to the shore that led to the pathway. I sighed, sinking down to sit on the leaves. Each crunch and crackle sounded and I no longer cared about the noise I'd made by crushing them beneath me.

Before I lost Catori, I would've never hesitated because I felt strong. Whatever strength that remained in me was just enough to get myself up and out of bed each morning. Hunting allowed me the focus and concentration I needed so that I wouldn't think about him. But it was no use. Things had changed since he was taken last winter. As a tribe, we would normally look out for one another. But ever since we lost Catori, we needed to account for every person in our tribe, especially when the sun went down. When winter approached and the days became shorter, there wasn't as much time for us to safely be outside. While we used to feast together as a tribe, we now ate in the solitude of our own homes. The togetherness that once was, no longer remained. Each morning, I would rush outside because that's the only time I felt I could truly breathe and be out in the open. Without fail every day, I would see the chief as he walked off toward the coast. Sometimes, his brother, Abornazine, would accompany him. But, most times...the chief wandered alone. One day, I chose to follow him, curious as to where he was going. Like the rabbit, he seemed to always be looking in the direction of the forbidden island. Even from the distance of the forest, I'd peek out and instantly recognize the suffering in his face. Annowan stared, hopeful…hopeful that he could someday get Catori back. I knew he had to have a part of him that believed it was possible. Without this dream and determination, neither of us would've found ourselves out of bed each day. I found myself doing the same, but just didn't know how that dream could turn into reality. Catori had made the ultimate sacrifice for me…for his tribe. It is something that I could never repay for the rest of my days. A selfless act that would never be forgotten. Yet…part of me felt as though he was still with me. Almost four seasons had passed by, yet we still heard the howls in the night; likely from Catori. Throughout the day, it was pure silence. No more laughter remained from everyone else and although Catori never thought he fit in, he seemed to be what held all of us together.

I headed closer to the shore, following the sounds of the steadily crashing waves. For the longest time, I wasn't able to even look at the island again. After venturing closer and closer, it didn't become any easier, but...the new life that I now faced became more real. Each morning, I had hoped to wake up from the nightmare that my life now was. The truth of it was a quick disappointment and so I continued believing I would someday wake up to the sound of Catori's voice. Avoiding the truths and dangers of the island caused my inability to cope with what truly had happened.

Each time I neared closer to the origins of the pain I felt every single day, it was as though something sharp pierced through my chest. Except this something was a pain I felt inside my body and could never rid myself of. The large boulder that Catori liked to lean up against still remained. The sound of crumbling leaves and humming snapped me out of my daze and I walked over to the boulder to see where the sound had come from. No animal or any other signs of life stood before me. The waves continued crashing against the shore and a blackbird with a patch of red on its wings flew off into the distance. I felt silly to always be on edge, as if someone or something was watching me at all times. I sighed, thinking of how anxious I had become. When I touched my hands to the sides of the boulder, my mind filtered through all the memories I shared with Catori out here. Not too long ago, Catori had been 'fishing' or trying to anyway...I laughed at how clumsy he was when everything he had brought had fallen over. When I saw he wasn't able to catch any fish despite being there for as long as he had been, I felt no choice but to assist him in bringing at least one fish back to the tribe.

The coarse outside of the rock felt harsh against the tips of my fingers. I pressed the entirety of my palm against it and closed my eyes, imagining he was still there. His back pressed against the height of the rock while I pushed into him; I would hold him in my arms for as long as I could if he was there. And for the longest time, I had thought of Catori as a big brother...until something in me switched and my mind thought up dreams of things that we could do together. Suddenly, a life without him no longer existed in my mind. There was no such thing. I had to get him back.

I reluctantly opened my eyes, wishing I could daydream for just a bit longer. Instead, there I was, staring longingly at the island that held the one person

I was meant for in this life. But it was still morning and no one would be looking for me quite yet. The sun drew higher in the sky as time passed by; I knew I'd have to head back soon or there would be a group searching for me. Just as there was in the very beginning, something seemed to draw me to the land. Despite the horrors I had dealt with, and the terror and loss that crippled me daily, the longing to be there again...was unavoidable.

Agisa

2

The calm of the ocean was something I always yearned to feel. I never hesitated when it came to taking every opportunity I could to be as close to it as possible. Life had a way of making sense when looking at the vast blue currents. Its deep hues of peace and serenity were tempting to walk right into. In the midst of the waves were the most mystical of places. It was almost as if nature meant for us to walk there, creating a path that would only open up at low tide. When I'd look out and stare at the beauty of the forbidden island, I always wondered and wished I could see what was within. I had come up with so many dreams in my mind for what it might be like. When you just walked on the shores, there was a deep forest within that many birds called their home. Snowy owls lurked there night and day, making their nests in the thick of the trees. From afar, the center looked like a giant bush one could easily get lost in. The simple thought of being there sent my mind imagining. The other side of the island could have the most incredible view of the ocean, with nothing else in sight. It would appear endless, revealing just how big our world truly was. I wondered what was beyond the boundless lengths of the deep blue as it extended past the point my mind could comprehend. Was this the only land there was? And did the water continue on endlessly?

Just then, I saw one of the women in our tribe walk out from the forest. She was holding a bow and arrow. When she turned, I could see her chestnut brown eyes and light brown hair that extended down to her waist. Aponi. I had always wondered where she ventured out to each morning when she wasn't with the rest of the women at the stream. Most times, I was too afraid to go up to her being that she went through so much. I didn't know what to say or where to begin, other than to tell her I was sorry for her loss. I crouched down to my knees, so that she didn't see me off in the distance, and continued to peek from the other side of the boulder. She looked like a lost girl there, standing still…motionless. I tried to follow her gaze that led right to the island. Eyes set for the walkway that led straight to it; she must have been tempted to go back. But how would she ever want to? Or was she replaying the horrors in her mind? The pathway was just before her at low tide and part of me thought she might take the chance to cross despite all that had happened. The others shared stories in private about a beast lurking there, and that very beast was the one that had taken the chief's son, Catori. No one was to speak of it, especially not around the chief. I still remembered when all the men came back, except for Catori. They had even somehow found Annowan's long-lost brother, which still puzzled me to this day. Yelling, screaming, begging...the men carried Aponi's body into the longhouse while everyone scrambled to help her any way they could. They were able to help ease her physical pain and bandage her wounds, but would likely never come close to ridding her of the pain she felt inside. It confused me how Aponi still looked toward the island, even though her friend had been taken. If that had happened to me, I wouldn't be caught anywhere near the island. But then again…here I was, crouched close by the path that led right there. Not knowing exactly what happened out there made me all the more curious. Coming to this place seemed to be unavoidable for the people of our tribe. Just as the waters always retreated to the sea, we, too, found ourselves there gathering the many things it offered our people. Neighboring tribes were not nearly as lucky when it came to having an abundance of shellfish, animals, and other fish available to them. Sometimes, we would trade with them…but it was very unlikely whilst each tribe tried to stick to their own territory. Although our tribe handled matters peacefully, the others didn't always…or at least those are the stories my grandfather passed down to me.

I crouched closer to the ground, rubbing against the leaves. When my knees pressed into them, they crumpled right when I had just tried to stay quiet. I squeezed my eyes, accepting my fate. She had to have heard me creeping around…I would just wait here until she'd come around and find me there. She would wonder what I was doing hiding behind the boulder. Or better…she'd likely ask why I was even there to begin with when the people of our tribe were warned again and again about coming as close as we were now to the pathway. As I held my hand over my mouth trying to quiet my strained breaths, I could hear her as her footsteps drew closer…confirming she might already know I am back here cowering like a defenseless rabbit.

I was never very good at hide-and-seek when I was young. Even in the most serious of moments, I'd often burst out in laughter. This was one of those times, but with the small chance she didn't know I was there…I had to continue hiding.

Aponi was out of sight for a short time, but the sounds of crumbling leaves faded until I realized she was walking away from the boulder. I breathed out a deep sigh, peeking around to see that she was already walking back inland through the forest. Finally, after all these years, I had won a game of hide-and-seek even though the other had no idea we were even playing. Gathering some of the dried blueberries and strawberries that I had been using before, I placed some into a bowl to smash down. My hands were a mess, and they stained anything else I touched. The lone piece of deerskin laid out perfectly against a rock. This was my usual space to paint, since it had a flat surface and was in direct sunlight. While I began pressing the colors from the dried fruits into it, I continuously looked up at the horizons to try to match the beautiful sight. Purple streaks left from the blueberries made me want to jump right into the painting I was making. I used pink for the skies just as they looked sometimes at sunrise with hints of yellow pressed in from some flowers I had collected. Guiding the colors into a half circle shape over the edges of the water, I was then able to take a darker color to add the island in the very center. As I took a step back after touching up a few more details, I half-smiled. It was a start, but nowhere close to capturing the beauty of nature around all of us. I wished I could find better colors to use so my painting reflected what I saw more accurately. Sunrise could be daunting for most to wake up and get out of bed. Especially in the cold of winter, warm blankets were much more appealing than the frigid air. But just one thought of what would be awaiting outside was more than worth it. Nature was something that could not be captured or controlled. That was one reason why it was so very beautiful. Even though some of the most graceful flowers would only last a short time, we grew to appreciate them all the more. When you have something unique, it is important for you to shower it with love and affection in hopes that you can make it last. No matter what, nothing lasts forever in its physical form...but the mark it has made on this world does. The pain of loss and death is surely unbearable, but it is better to have experienced love and beauty than nothing at all.

I added a path of a lighter blue tone over what I had already painted and it seemed to darken, revealing various shades of gray as soon as I painted more purple over it. Brushing my fingertip from the sun all the way down to the mainland, I made sure to keep this same shade. Instead of it going to the island, I changed it a little bit and made it seem like you could follow that directly to the sun. I stood back and looked at the actual pathway that the waves crashed up against and then back down at my painting. I felt I should have kept it the same as in life since the pathway did lead to the island…but there was more meaning in this. Even when one traveled alone or had to journey through life on their own, they would still find a path that would lead them toward the light. The light could represent the beginning or end of one's life when their spirit came into this world or remained here to watch over others. It could also be the balance that life gave when someone needed that bit of hope to keep them going. The dark purples showed the darkness throughout their journey, but the sun at the end revealed the inevitable light. They just had to keep going in order to reach it.

I stepped back again and smiled at my work. Although the meager amount of colors I had couldn't quite display exactly what I wanted, I began creating a list in my mind of the things I could gather in order to make some new shades. I stayed there for a while longer to make sure the painting could dry a little and held the very corner of it, collecting my supplies so I could walk back. As soon as I slung my bag over my shoulder, out of the very corner of my eye, I could faintly see something moving on the island. Despite its distance, the more I squinted...the more I was able to clearly make out a man who paced alone. Blinking my eyes several times, I tried to snap myself out of it.

"Agisa...you are losing your mind," I whispered to myself while my eyes were still shut. "You're going to open your eyes and it will all be in your head." I clenched my jaws, fearful of reopening my eyes, since I didn't know what I would see. I hoped I was just tired and daydreaming... One by one, I lifted my eyelids and looked left...right...all over. No one. There was no one. The hair stood up on my arms as a deep fear washed over me, similar to the waves that would completely conceal the path. When I turned to leave, I kept looking behind me to make sure that no one was following me.

Every crackle of the leaves beneath my feet or slightest movement an animal would make startled me. I sped up my pace and finally reached home to drop off my things so I could try to start this day over...hopefully forgetting what I had seen.

Aponi

3

If anyone caught me standing out there so close to the walkway that led right up to the island, I would've surely been tied down for my own good. The tribe stayed far away to the point they haven't so much as glanced at the forbidden land since that day. Waking up before the sun each morning became a routine as I went out again and again to hunt with my bow. Leaving later than I had, the others would find out, and I had no idea what they would say about a woman hunting like the men normally did. Hunting gave me the strength I needed to get through each day. I could feel a deep wound inside me I knew would never heal, but as long as I diverted my attention, worries seemed to get pushed to the back of my mind. And that short amount of time at peace was worth it.

Leaves crunched with each step I took on my way back toward our homes. The morning calls of birds just waking up were bound to awaken the others soon, if it hadn't already. The stillness of the cool air sent chills down my back. As I drew closer to home, it made me want to turn back all the more…realizing that I wasn't actually going home, but instead, away from it. Being at sea was my true home and when I felt most at peace. It also made me feel that much closer to Catori, even though his body was now taken over by an uncontrollable beast. I walked past the wigwam my family slept in and questioned whether or not I should go inside and act like I had been sleeping this entire time. It would likely not work, but the warmth of my bed seemed to lure me in. Just before I turned to enter, I shook off the feeling of crawling back into bed and continued further down toward the stream where women of the tribe commonly met to wash clothes.

"Hey, Aponi! Wait up!" a familiar voice called out. I stopped in my tracks and hoped they hadn't seen me coming from the shores. I sighed a breath of relief at Mato's dopey grin spread from ear to ear as he approached. His shaggy hair was still the same as it always was, even when we were just growing up. For some reason, it was a bunch of different lengths and always looked like he had just rolled out of bed.

"Hello." I continued walking, and he followed beside me like some lost pup. Women's voices rang out louder when we drew closer to the stream. They liked to sing together, which was something I never was a part of. Never had I been a part of the group that sang their words aloud for others to hear.

"What were you doing up so early?" he asked, ignoring the others.

"Just went for a walk." I was telling the truth…

"So early and all by yourself?" The worry in his voice didn't surprise me. It wasn't typical, especially in the late fall, for us to go out alone. Animals were desperate for food at this time of year, since they knew it would no longer be available in the cold of winter.

"I'll be fine. No need to worry," I assured him.

"I could go with you if you want," he suggested. I was grateful for the care he showed, but at times, he was like an annoying little brother that I never wished to have. I couldn't seem to get him to stop following me, but decided on ignoring him instead and hoped he would grow bored and just walk away at some point. Leaves rustled around us from the other people in our tribe as they walked around. During the day, everyone was busy at work getting chores done and preparing for winter. I could still hear Mato's footsteps as they trailed behind me. Voices in the distance continued to appear louder the closer we came. The quietness of dawn seemed like just a few moments ago and I longed to be back there in my own company; the person the tribe saw me as was no longer here. They just didn't quite realize it yet. I began walking faster and waved at the other women, taking a heap of clothes in my arms and heading over to an opening in the stream that wasn't in use by the others.

"Hey, come on!" Mato grabbed my arm, causing some clothes to fall to the ground.

"Okay, what do you want, Mato?" I plopped the rest of the clothes that remained in my arms down, not caring much anymore since I would have to wash them anyway. When I crossed my arms over my chest in annoyance, I couldn't help but feel sorry for him deep down. The eager look in his eyes…so full of hope and promise. He was one of the few that still seemed to see the light in this world. He wasn't damaged like the rest of us. When you have seen so many horrors in your life and can't possibly shut them out, no matter how hard you try, you learn to accept life for what it was.

"Ok, you can't tell anyone. You promise?" he asked.

I nodded, and he continued. "You've talked to Agisa before, right?"

"Yes…" I answered. Suddenly, the conversation was turning elsewhere and I couldn't be more glad. For the longest time, the focus had been on me and how fragile I was. Don't stay out too late, make sure you have someone with you at all times… Now that other things were in the light… I felt I could breathe a little easier. I looked over at Agisa, who was much further down than where Mato and I stood. Agisa's raven colored hair was tied back in a long braid, trailing down to her waist. Her face was much more rounded than mine and she appeared to be healthier than I. I hadn't taken proper care of myself and had slimmed down to where I barely fit in my clothes as they loosely draped over me. Agisa wore a long dress made of deerskin that came down to her ankles and had brown frills that dangled off the edges. I gazed back into her black eyes at the same time she had been glancing over at us. As soon as she saw that I noticed, she quickly looked away.

"Oh...you like her, huh?" I grinned over at Mato, who kneeled beside me in an attempt to hide from her. Dipping each shirt into the water with some herbs, I couldn't help but feel amused by Mato's childish ways. He was now a grown man and could no longer hide like he could as a little boy.

"No, I just wanted to know if you and her were friends," he insisted.

"Mato...how long have we known each other?" I asked, knowing full well the answer.

"Fine." He shrugged his shoulders and looked down at the dirt—anything but locking eyes with mine. "I might like her."

"So then go over to her; she's right there," I said.

"I don't know enough about her." He shook his head; his dark shaggy hair fell over one side of his face. He quickly tied it back, as I could see the sweat stream down from his forehead. It was a perfectly cool day, so he must have been nervous, to say the least.

"Well, how else do you think you're going to find out more?" I left the clothes to soak in the water and pulled Mato up from where he just kneeled, guiding him toward Agisa, who continued washing her clothes in the water.

"Where are we going?" he asked and as soon as he realized, he protested by planting both of his feet in the ground.

"You act like I'm bringing you toward your death. Come on," I said, a little bit too loud for his liking. His feet remained planted; stubborn boy. Agisa must've seen and heard all the commotion since she was no longer washing any clothes. She looked almost as scared as the rabbit had this morning; unknowing of what we were about to say or do. It was very likely she had never spoken to a boy before, being that she spent the majority of her time with the women harvesting and cleaning.

"Are you two okay?" she asked. Mato and I just looked at one another and I realized I was still yanking him toward her while he had his arms crossed in a pouty attempt to rid himself of me.

"Yes."

"No."

We both said at the same time. Agisa chuckled and I could see the wall she had put up break down just a little bit. I let go of Mato's arm since I seemed to have gotten what I wanted; for them to confront one another.

"He found himself here with the other women while the men are out hunting. He's a silly man, and I was just showing him back," I said.

"I'm right here, you know," Mato grunted.

"Oh hey, do you think maybe you could show him back to the longhouse? I can do your clothes with mine," I said as I ignored him.

"Wait—" Mato was just about to blurt out some excuse to get out of it. I never knew him to be as shy as this, and it was quite entertaining.

"You'd do that for me? Wow, thanks! Yeah, I'll show Mato back. I'd think he'd know the way though…" Agisa said.

"You'd think," I answered back and could hear Mato's annoyed scoff. As I scooped up her clothes in my hands, I squeezed them out and couldn't help but laugh. Annoying him was a fun way to pass the time, but my true worry had a way of creeping back to the center of my mind, dismissing any joy I could possibly feel. I felt a great deal of guilt wash over me as I stay here laughing away and living a somewhat normal life. The inevitable thought came back to Catori, who was caged like some animal on the island that we would never set foot on again. Denial came in unavoidable waves, pressing me to still have hope to save him…to bring him back.

Agisa

4

When I saw the others, I was relieved and felt much more safe. Being alone was something I was used to, but not in the horrors of the unknown. For the longest time, I felt the men could protect us in our tribe. But after what happened to Catori—the chief's own son—I realized just how much we were all in danger. And now, I definitely saw someone on the island. It haunted me beyond reason. My heart raced, but seeing the others made me feel like it could've just been something else on the island. After all, I only saw the movement once and then it vanished. Shaking my head back and forth as if to shake out all the bad thoughts, I tried to push my worries away. It was just some animal or something. It had to be. When I neared the stream, there was a pile of clothes waiting for me to wash. This would help take my mind off it all... The women of our tribe all worked together as they sang by the stream. Their voices were soothing while they sang the same song of our people that we all knew as well as we knew the paths of the forest.

Most would hum and sing, but others preferred to get their work done on their own in the peace and tranquility nature had to offer. I enjoyed singing to their melodies since it helped the work get done that much faster. Deep down, I longed to finish so I could get back to painting. Not that painting was off limits to me, but the places I would go were far from the tribe's comfortable boundaries. It was especially dangerous for someone to go on their own after all that happened. I could hear voices talking and quickly realized they were coming toward me. Part of me felt as though one of them said my name, Agisa. I glanced over and found Aponi not too far away from where I was kneeling. She was just starting to do her own clothes and must've taken a bit longer coming back than I. Beside her stood one of the tribesmen, Mato. His shaggy hair was just as it had always been when we were all growing up as children. Aponi always hung around the group of boys while I stayed with the other girls and oftentimes, rushed home to draw and paint on my own.

Aponi looked over at me, and we locked eyes. It looked like she wanted to come over to me and talk about something. My hands instantly felt clammy in fear that she caught me out there too by the shores. I broke my gaze and turned back to the clothes that laid damp in my hands, trying to continue on so I could leave sooner. The voices continued and eventually drew even closer to the point they felt as though they were right on top of me. I looked to my left to find Aponi and Mato standing beside me. Doe-eyed—which is what I was named for—I just glanced up and waited for my secret to be revealed. They didn't say anything, but for some reason, Aponi was practically dragging Mato over toward me. What could he have to do with any of this? Was he there too, by the water? I asked if they were okay and they both said yes and no at the same time. It was all kind of funny; I couldn't help but laugh as I dropped the clothes down in the water and sat back, holding my belly. Aponi explained that Mato somehow got to the stream and wanted to join us in cleaning our clothes? It was an excuse even I couldn't believe and still didn't seem to answer how he made it over there. I was just glad Aponi didn't bring up what she may have seen this morning, although it would only cause more questions about her if she ever told anyone. So I guessed in a way I was safe and didn't have to worry...but still. I agreed to guide Mato back even though I was sure he knew the way, but Aponi promised to do my clothes as well. I would be heading back to the wigwams to gather my painting materials, so this worked out perfectly.

As Mato and I headed away from the women in our tribe, their voices trailed in the distance and silence surrounded both of us. Other than the crackling of leaves beneath our feet and a few crows cawing in the distance, we did not voice a sound. I wondered which of us would break the silence and thought of the melodies he would play by the fires at night. I always enjoyed when he brought out his music. Ever since Catori was lost from our tribe, we no longer had fires together and the only time that the tribe shared was during our chores. I decided to start asking some of the many unanswered questions I had.

"So, you don't know where we live anymore?" I asked playfully.

"I do—" he replied. "It's just that I had wanted to ask you something."

"Me?" I stopped where I stood and turned to face him. Mato jerked his head to the left, allowing his hair to fall to the side so his eyes weren't covered as much.

His broad shoulders were enough to make me feel safe right there, but it was more of a brotherly type of safe.

"Well, I wanted to know if you would like to get to know one another a little bit more. Maybe we can just go for a nice walk."

"What are we doing now?" I asked, but felt like it came off a little bit harsh. It was an honest question, though.

"No, like…get to know one another. You know?" he asked.

"Oh sure, I would love to make more friends!" I exclaimed. I knew he likely wanted more since he was singling me out, but it was best not to lead him down a path that was unlikely to have a destination.

"Yeah, friends. Okay, that sounds good!" he said, but looked down at the ground as we continued walking. The air around us suddenly felt sad and depressing.

"Would you be able to bring your music sometime, too? It's been so long since we all sat at a fire and just enjoyed one another," I mentioned. He stopped looking down at the ground.

"Yeah, you know what? Even though the chief doesn't come out very often other than to hunt, it doesn't mean we can't all get together. That's a really good idea. We should."

I nodded, and we continued on. As the wigwams came into view, he walked off toward the main longhouse which was in the center of our smaller homes. I saw a group of women walk off and Mato's eyes seemed distracted by them. It looked like he was already onto the next without wasting much time; I didn't feel as bad anymore.

"Hey, thanks for getting me out of cleaning clothes!" I called over to him after he'd begun to go the other way.

"Sure thing!" He turned back and smiled. "Let's plan a fire for tonight. How does that sound?" he asked.

"Perfect! Invite Aponi and I'll tell the others."

Aponi

5

I spent the rest of the day avoiding anyone I could and trying my best to get back home before anyone else could deter me elsewhere and ask questions. The thing about home was that sometimes it was even worse since there was no escaping Mother when she repeatedly asked if I was okay. Mother and I would often sit beside Father in silence as we ate. It was depressing to be indoors, and I wanted to just walk around and get some air, but being alone out at night wasn't allowed. Looking at Mother was like looking into a mirror of my own reflection if it weren't for my skin that was much lighter than hers. Father's bushy eyebrows outlined his dark brown eyes as he stared back at me. I missed the days when he would joke about how thankful he was I didn't end up having his bushy eyebrows. Having them both here with me gave me a slight bit of warmth that I had been lacking—even with the silence. They never knew what to say anymore, especially after nearly losing me. We all felt a bit of guilt for being able to eat together while Catori's family remained broken. Father was there when the tribesmen found me and brought me back to the mainland. His face filled with a shock and horror that I had never witnessed before.

"Where do you go each morning, A?" Father asked, using his nickname for me. I could feel myself sinking down and hoped the grounds would open up so I could hide instead of having to come up with an excuse. I had thought I was quiet enough each morning that they didn't know.

"Your mother and I are worried about you. You show up to harvest and clean much later than the other women and we never know where you come from," he explained further, as I couldn't seem to open my mouth or find the words. It felt like it had been sewn shut. They glanced at one another, then back at me, expecting me to say something that would ease their worries.

"I just need time to get some air alone, that's all." I couldn't lie to them, but I didn't have to reveal everything. Father knew I could use a bow and arrow. He was one of the people who taught me aside from Catori, but he didn't want me letting Mother know. He had already gotten up and walked around to me. When he placed a firm hand on my shoulder, I stood up and hugged him. No matter how old I got, I always felt like a child again in his arms.

"What kind of hug is that?" He would always joke.

"It's a hug."

"You can do better than that!" he challenged as I hugged him tighter, likely making no difference since he was much larger than me. I felt him lift me off the ground and smiled just like I would when I was a little girl and saw the grounds from much higher.

"Cho," Mother said his short name for Chogan. In our culture, it meant blackbird. He was named for the red-winged blackbird that would frequently appear near the shore. It was seen as a guardian spirit in a way for many. We both looked over at Mother as she stood up and walked over toward us. "Why don't you two go out on a walk together in the morning?"

"Does that sound okay to you, A?" he asked, letting me go. He crossed his arms over his chest while he waited for my response. Bushy eyebrows lifted as if to silently beg 'please' without actually saying anything at all.

"Yeah, that's okay. Just like old times, right?" I thought back to when Father first taught me to hunt. Oftentimes, Catori would accompany us on our journeys. It was a time I wished I could blink my eyes and wake up to.

A knock came from outside. Both of them looked at me and then at the door as if the knock was for me and couldn't possibly have been for any other reason. I shrugged my shoulders because I hadn't the slightest idea either of who it could have been. Everyone else in the tribe would've been with their own families eating before they went to bed for the night. Father stood and walked outside. In just a few moments, he was back and I could see Mato and Agisa peeking through the doorway behind Father. What were these two up to? Perhaps trying to set them up together wasn't a good plan of mine.

"Your friends want you to come to a fire with them," Father said.

"What? Okay then…" I said, remaining seated as I knew full well what Father would likely say next.

"You know how I feel about you going out at night…" he said, still standing before Mato and Agisa while they eagerly waited in the doorway.

"As long as she is with her friends and not alone, I don't see why not?" Mother asked and told at the same time. She looked almost as doe eyed as Agisa. Father took a deep breath and looked over at me, then to my friends again. She put him in a difficult place because now, if he said no…it was all going to be his fault. Little did he know I didn't really mind whether I went or not.

"You two better not bring her back late and don't let her out of your sight," he said. I wasn't expecting to leave and reluctantly stood up, staring at my warm bed that I would have to come back to much later. Part of me hoped for Father to say no, but I guess they were ready for me to live a somewhat normal life, if that was even possible at this point.

"Yes!" they both said in unison. I slowly walked over and faced Father and Mother when I was just about out the door.

"I will see you soon. Thank you for letting me go," I said while I shoved my head through a fur covering since the nights were getting colder as fall came to an end. I fully breathed in and out when I got outside. I wished I could spend much more time in the cool, night air...but at the same time, I wished to be in the warmth. Either side couldn't win at this. The darkness of the night caused my curiosity to wonder of what else there was to see out here. I wished I could bring a bow and arrow with me so I could use it to sneak up on prey in the night.

"So...what is this random plan for escape all about?" I asked, confused. It seemed this was Agisa's idea since she spoke first. Mato just continued walking and held a torch that he had lit before. It was much too dark to to rely on the moonlight in its entirety. We would've never found our way without the torch.

"We were talking about how we haven't had a fire in so long and thought it would be a good idea to get together…you know, for all of us." She continued walking.

"So we are having a fire, then?" I asked.

"Yeah, why not?!" Mato exclaimed and started walking toward the longhouse. In the cold, the tribe used a small fire pit that was in the middle of the main house where we used to feast. There was a small hole in the roof of the house that we could cover whenever we were not using it. This allowed the smoke to leave and not stay within. We couldn't forget to uncover it or else we would choke ourselves out of air. We definitely didn't want that tonight.

"Okay…and who else is coming?" I felt like I was the mother of the group, looking after all the details of our plans and trying to figure out if everything would work out. They both just shrugged their shoulders, and I laughed at our small little party that we had here.

"The less to start with, the better. Next time, we can invite more people. We just thought it would be nice with just us for now," Agisa answered before heading into the longhouse.

"Well, you guys seem to be getting along great…huh?" I asked.

"We're both just excited about doing this finally!" Mato said. They looked at one another and smiled. Something caught my eye on the other side of the room.

It was the lavender that was likely untouched since I last used it. The smell was the most calming to me and relieved any bad feelings I had. It used to, anyway…I hadn't used it since the last night the entire tribe was together. I began walking over toward it to put it on when I traced the scars on my arms with my fingertips. They were mostly healed by now, but I couldn't help but flinch every time I looked down at them. There was no physical pain anymore, but the memory still remained. At times, I thought this was a worse pain than any physical one could be, since there was no way to see or bandage the pain I felt inside. It was very unlikely it would heal anyway. Instead, I just somehow managed to push it to the back of my mind so I could attempt at living again.

"Ooh, good idea! The lavender will be perfect!" Agisa said from the center of the room. They must have been watching me. I peered over my shoulder and saw Mato as he lifted Agisa up to slide the small piece of bark over from the top of the roof, revealing the night sky above. A stroke of moonlight was let in and the small stream of smoke from the lavender filled the room in a fragrance I thought I had long forgotten.

Agisa
6

Aponi was someone I had looked up to all my life. We barely spoke, but she was so different from the rest of us. Anytime we were in a group, she would lead the rest of us…even the boys. For a long time, I felt intimidated by her and even scared to speak to her, not knowing if what I would say was the right thing or if I would only embarrass myself. But on the day the chief brought her back as her body lay limp on the ground and all the women swarmed to her aid to attempt at helping her…I no longer felt intimidated by her. She was just like the rest of us, but now the harsh edge that she had no longer remained. What we all saw was what we felt inside: scared and lost. Seeing someone so incredible be broken down to their lowest point possible awakened me in a way. It showed me none of us are perfect. Anyone…no matter how powerful, can be broken down. I thought of the flowers I sometimes mashed up to use in my paintings and how they were once so beautiful, but could be used in many different ways. I couldn't imagine what Aponi was even going through, but knew that she, too—like my flowers— could find a painting to be a part of. One she would never grow sick of living within and could somehow cure her brokenness.

"Want to get on my shoulder so we can open up the top a bit for the smoke to let out?" Mato's voice snapped me out of my thoughts.

"Oh yeah, yes," I answered. He put his hands on my waist and lifted me high. The effortless way in which he picked me up slightly stirred something in me I hadn't felt before. My stomach flipped as I was in his muscular embrace. Butterflies relentlessly fluttered about. I shook my head, knowing full well I was not interested in Mato in that way, but still couldn't help the feeling that now blossomed in my heart.

"Just move that piece of bark over, but not too much. We have to make sure we can push it back when we are done." I followed what he said and right when I pressed my fingers to the roof, I could feel the piece move up. Gliding it over a bit, I dropped my arms to my side when I finished. Looking down at Mato, he was staring straight at my chest as I reached up. When he saw I caught what he had been looking at, he tore his eyes off me and pretended to be watching something else.

"All set!" I said, feeling his arms guide me back down and as my feet met the ground, I could still feel his hands on my waist. Blinking a few times, I looked up into his soft eyes. Something in me arose that I hadn't felt before and I questioned what it would feel like to give him a chance.

"Are we going to have a fire or what?" Aponi asked, spooking us both out of our gaze.

"Yes, just going to start the fire. You two sit around and I'll light it," Mato said, smiling before he went off to spark the fire pit in the center. Aponi and I both sat close to one another. While Mato worked on lighting the fire, I couldn't help but think about the shores and wondered what Aponi had been doing over there.

"Be right back. I've got to go get some wood from just outside," he called.

"So...do you like him?" Aponi asked something I hadn't even been thinking about.

"Who? Mato?" I asked.

She nodded.

"Well, he's a nice guy..." I shifted where I sat to get more comfortable.

"I think it would be worth a try," she suggested.

"I don't know... I mean, he is good looking. He is nice, too. But I just don't feel a real connection there." I hesitated and tried to keep my voice down so he wouldn't hear me on the off chance he was on his way back inside. She ran her fingers through her hair, tugging out any knots, and brought it all to the front.

When she lifted her hand to her head, the deep scar on her wrist showed and I nearly jumped at the sight of it.

"What's wrong?" she asked and seeing her scar reminded me of earlier this morning in our encounter. At this point, I realized she couldn't have seen me. I felt no choice but to bring it up and see what she said, even if it meant her knowing I was out there, too.

"Aponi...I think I saw you by the shore earlier," I finally managed to say. A long sigh came from her lips as she intently looked right at me.

"I was just going for a walk," she said.

"You use a bow and arrow?" I asked further. I knew I was being annoying, but was also so intrigued.

"What were you doing by the shore?" She changed the topic and I should've expected as much, but wished she would have answered my question first.

"I sometimes go out there to paint because the island is so pretty," I said before I could take it back, realizing she likely didn't feel the same about it.

"The island is not a pretty scene." Aponi looked down. I readjusted, not knowing what to say to her. I felt like I had been ignorant about how she felt about the island.

"I know you have been through a lot on that land…it wasn't right to say…" I instantly felt bad for the horrors she went through.

"No, you're right, Agisa. The island has always been beautiful to me. too, but when I actually experienced its terrors, I could never think of it as a beautiful place again. All I see is blood when I look at it," she sighed. I slid closer to her and hugged her as we sat there.

"I couldn't even imagine."

"Don't even try," she said.

"Well, why do you go to the shore to look out at it, then?" I asked. If I had been through just a portion of what she had, I wouldn't want to look at the place ever again.

"As far as I'm concerned, the only beautiful thing that remains there is Catori..." she replied, sighing.

"So, you think he's still there?" I asked, curious. I wanted to tell her about what I saw on the island...or what I thought I saw and quickly dismissed.

"I know he's still there," she answered and Mato came back, stopping us from our conversation we had just been having. There was a silent agreement between the two of us right then to never share what we just had with any other soul. No one would understand unless they were in her position. The fact that Catori might still be out there was likely all the hope she needed to get her through each day. I was scared for her that she may try to venture out to the island to get him back. She would put herself into a position that was even worse than she had come back in.

"You get the wood you needed?" Aponi asked him. Mato had a pile in his arms that would've likely made me fall to the ground if I tried holding the same amount. He nodded and plopped it all down in the pit before us. The thud made me jump, but I felt like I was already spooked from what Aponi had just told me. Mato tried to spark a couple of rocks together with the sticks a few times until one finally lit. The fiery glow spread from that one small initial spark to a few other sticks that lay close by. It was amazing how fast it was able to spread.

Mato sat down beside us as soon as he was content with how the fire looked. Resting back on his forearms, he watched the fire engulfed the other pieces of wood. I did the same and took in the smell of lavender that filled the room. It seemed to have been a long day for him and I couldn't help but feel tired as I would've usually been asleep by then.

"So…anyone want to share a story?" he asked.

"Does it have to be real?" I wondered. He shook his head. I glanced over at Aponi. It seemed she would not be talking anytime soon. She looked to be in a lull from the lavender.

"I have a story…" I said. It was easy for me because I would think about my paintings since each one of them had a message that was conveyed. I continued when no one else volunteered. "There was a woman who walked out each night so that she could paint the moon. Every night, she would sneak out and the few times she was caught, others would tell her not to go alone. They warned her of the creatures that lurked within the night ...”

“Ooh, this is getting scary,” Mato said. Aponi looked intrigued and leaned in.

“On the night of the full moon, she walked out despite what the others said. She planned to paint a new picture that she had never done before. Hours had passed, but she waited for the perfect moment. When the moon neared its highest point in the sky, the woman began painting away, vigorously. The luminous patch of white in the sky had finally reached the top, and that was when she finally finished her painting. She looked at it and noticed something peculiar that wasn't evident before. A distinct glow seemed to seep out of it unlike anything she had ever seen..." I stopped, swallowing hard. This was a dream I had many times, and saying it aloud was like bringing it to life.

"Oh, you can't stop it there! What was it?!" Aponi shouted, to my surprise. I smiled because I wasn't even at the best part yet.

"It was so beautiful that even though she knew the paint had to dry, she was drawn to touch it. As soon as her fingertips brushed against the deerskin that she had painted on, its entirety sucked her in. Unexpected, she had no one to call to for help and nothing to reach out and hold on to. When every last bit of her no longer remained in the outside world, she realized the blessing and curse at the same time. She forever lived in the painting of the most beautiful moon she had ever seen…in a land that was endless and full of wonder."

"Where do you come up with these things?!" Mato said. "All I would've had was the story of my walk this morning!" Aponi and I both started laughing uncontrollably. Mato could be very funny. We spent a little while longer sharing silly stories and eventually went off to walk Aponi to her wigwam she shared with her mother and father. Mato walked me to mine since his was right beside it.

"Hey, thanks for coming out tonight. This is the most fun I have had in a while." I looked up at him, moonlight glistening on us.

"Let's do it again." He wrapped his arms around me in a tight embrace that, for some reason, I didn't want to leave, but at the same time I knew the longer I stayed in it…the more difficult it would be for me to leave. He smiled and kissed me on the forehead, waving as he walked off to his home.

Aponi

7

Water trickled down from above, splashing onto my face. I tried to pull the blanket over my head, but realized it had been getting in through the roof of our home. The darkness that crept through the windows revealed the inevitable gloom that continued to surround us all. I ran toward the bowls and grabbed one of the largest ones I could find to place on my bed so it could collect water and salvage the remnants of what once was my warm, dry bed.

"Mother? Father?" I called out, wondering why they hadn't heard me already or even noticed the rain. There was no answer. The painfully quiet room made me feel more alone than I truly was. I walked over to find them still fast asleep in their bed. They were calmly lying there, deeply breathing in and out. They didn't seem to hear me, even though I had screamed their names. The bowl had almost filled completely and was on its way to overflowing. As I scurried over, a strong wind blew the door open and still, both Mother and Father remained sound asleep. I quickly replaced the bowl and headed outside. The cool air rushed towards me, pushing the door open even more. I closed it behind me and edged further out into the night, unknowing of what I would find. It had been so long since I'd been out here alone and part of me felt fearful, but the other part missed the feeling of venturing out. Off in the distance, I could hear the owls in the trees as they called to one another. Aside from their calls, the rain continued to trickle down from above, each drop crashing onto me. A branch cracked in the distance and if it weren't for the moonlight, I wouldn't have been able to see a thing. Stumbling further out into the night—something seemed to draw me away from home, although I knew I was exactly where I should be. The rain stopped, but my hair was still damp and clung to my skin, trailing down my back. A cloud must have drifted over the moon, as there was no longer any light to be my guide.

Darkness swallowed me whole, and I backed up, hoping to reach home again. The more I moved, the farther away I felt until I walked into something stiff and its warm arms wrapped around me. It was a familiar warmth I hadn't felt in a long time.

"Is it you?" I asked, blind to the world that surrounded us. I could feel him turn me around so we were facing one another and despite my inability to actually see him, I knew exactly who was there with me. Pressing my hands to his bare chest, I embraced him, wishing to never let go.

"Aponi." His voice was full of pain, but still there. In the next moment, I could see the moonlight shine off his face and those sweet, deep brown eyes that I had been missing for far too long. His absence in my life made it seem like he was nothing but a mere dream.

"Don't go. Please stay," I begged, more worried about keeping him here than trying to figure out how he got back in the first place.

"I can't…" He pressed his lips together and gently touched his forehead to mine. "Whatever happens…you need to stay away."

"Catori," I said and saw my breath in the frigid air before me. Nothing else remained other than the dark night as I was once again alone and my hands pressed into the sides of my home. It was as if I was imagining things. I walked back in and tried to shake it off, but I could have sworn he was truly there. I didn't know how, but I felt him. He was there.

In the next moment, I felt the warm fur blankets of my bed as they wrapped around me. I woke up in a sweat despite fall's frigid morning air. It was as if I never even went to sleep, but somehow the night had come and gone…and the world around continued on as if nothing had happened. All around me, there wasn't even the slightest hint as to the rainfall that nearly flooded my bed last night. It must have all been a dream. I looked around and thought about how it likely had little effect on anyone else as much as it did to me. That was the most gut-reaching part of all of this. People partook in their normal daily activities and eventually…any mention of Catori would fade from existence. That was my biggest fear. I couldn't let him die off and in my heart, I knew he was there with me— dream or not. I pushed the blanket down toward my feet and winced at the sunlight that streamed in through the window.

"Thought you would sleep all day! Finally!" Father called out from the other side of our home. Mother must have already gone to harvest any remaining vegetables with the other women. I was surprised

Father waited so long since the men usually got up at dawn to go hunting. That's just after I would make my escape out to do some hunting of my own.

"Is it that late already?" I asked, remaining in bed. For some reason, I couldn't get my legs off the bed. I felt glued to it and just didn't want to leave. Father didn't answer and instead, laid my bow and arrows beside me that I normally kept hidden under my bed. That got me up right away.

"Let's go; I'll meet you out there soon," he said.

"Okay." I scurried over to change the clothes I was wearing. A beige dress that Mother had made from the deerskin that Father brought home after one of his hunts was the easiest thing to throw over my head. I quickly slung the bag of bows over my shoulder and held the arrow in my other hand, finally leaving to meet Father.

"Stand back." His arm extended out over the front of my body that blocked me from stepping any farther. Instead of the men of our tribe already being out hunting, they stood beside our home in a group. I peered out over his shoulder while he was acting as a wall in between me and whatever had been the focus of almost the entire tribe.

"Father, what's—" I began to ask and was quickly shushed by him and some of the other men nearby. He pushed me back toward the house and just before I went in, I was able to catch a glimpse of several men on horses. Sometimes, our tribe would use horses…but since we lived so close by to the shores, we did not have much need to go very far. But these men…these men were not part of our tribe. The one in the very front had the most pale shade of white skin I had ever seen before and his straight but rigid nose, along with the firm crease of his lips, looked nowhere as soft as the appearances of the people in our tribe. One of the biggest differences was that he had much lighter hair pulled back in a ponytail. He was nothing like anyone I had ever seen.

Agisa

8

A tall pile of clothes nearly reached above my head; I could barely see where I was even going. If it weren't for my routine of taking the same path time and time again, I would've had no idea where I was headed. The tree roots laid about the ground proved to be the biggest obstacle in my way, although they made things more interesting. In the distance, I thought I heard a horse's hooves click as it trotted through the woods. I froze in my path when I saw the pack of horses before me as they trekked through. I was completely out in the open, but dropped the clothes where I stood and scampered behind the nearest tree for coverage.

One peek out from the tree showed me that these were people our tribe had never seen before. There were times other tribes came into contact with our own, but the features of each were strikingly similar. Men and women both either had shades of brown or black hair. Our eyes oftentimes mirrored that. This tribe...shared no similarities with ours. The men that rode the horses had fair skin and much lighter hair. There were some that even had white, curly hair. It looked as though it was fake somehow, which I had no idea why someone would want to put white hair on top of their own natural locks. A deep fear instantly arose in me that these men may not be so good after all. I wondered where they came from and what they were doing here. With the tribe's vulnerable state, there was no knowing what could be taken from us or worse…

As they drew further away from me, I followed behind and tiptoed from tree to tree so I could get a closer look but still remain hidden. They came all the way to the main longhouse and stopped their horses in the middle of our homes. A man in the front who surprisingly did not wear a wig jumped down from his horse and walked up to the chief, Annowan. It was even more alarming to see that he finally came out of his home at a time other than for hunting. His eyes looked drawn, as if he hadn't slept in days. Head down, a long way away from the times when his broad shoulders and powerful gaze would deter anyone from trying to steal anything from us. Where there was once a man full of strength, now stood one who looked as though even the wind could knock him down. I hoped Aponi was right about Catori. If there was even a slight chance he could come back, it would bring the life back to our tribe.

As I snuck closer, the man who was no longer on his horse spoke to Annowan. The words that came out of his mouth sounded like gibberish and were from a language I had never heard before. Annowan didn't seem to understand him either, and the man took the hint, walking back to his horse. Just when I thought he was leaving, he continued walking instead toward a pile that trailed behind the horse. It was pulling a long tray that had various items in it hidden under a blanket. As soon as he turned, I could see his beautiful, pale face. Light hair was tied back, but some strands poked out as they clung to the sides of his face. His dark eyebrows clashed with the rest of his appearance; especially his eyes. They were a new sight that I knew I would never grow tired of. I wished to get a closer look, but from where I hid, I could see they contained the lightest of blues that I had only been able to capture when the sunlight hit the sea in the morning. The light that reflected made it appear to be dream-like. I couldn't stop staring at him as he rummaged through whatever lay beneath the blanket. A vibrant red shone out from the wooden basket and revealed something new to my eyes. It piqued my curiosity, wondering what it was. The man walked over to Annowan and handed a red ball to him. His brother, Abornazine, stood beside him. While Annowan hesitated, refusing to take it in his hand, Abornazine was just about to take it instead when the unfamiliar man pulled it toward his mouth. To my surprise, he bit it. Juices seeped out from the sides as he held the red thing out again.

Annowan took it and bit into it as the man just had. He then handed it to his brother to take a bite. His face said it all as soon as he took one bite. Annowan's eyes lit up, and he even took another bite right after. I heard the man laugh as if this was what he expected. The chief smiled at him. I wondered what this unfamiliar group of people expected in return for their kind gift. The man pointed to the red thing that Annowan still held in his hand, no longer red…instead, a very light shade of yellow all around it.

"Apple," he said to Annowan.

"Apple?" Annowan echoed back, and the man nodded, handing him the entire basket of what he called apples. I was ready to go over there and try one myself, but knew I couldn't be caught. Especially in this kind of situation where both sides had no idea whether or not we could trust one another. Annowan walked back with a fur covering that he handed to the man, who shivered where he stood. He placed it up and over his head, then put out his hand. Annowan just stood there and looked at him, but eventually, the man took his hand and shook it. What an odd thing to do.

When he turned around to get back on his horse, I felt his eyes lock on mine. He saw me as my head peeked out from behind one of the trees that I thought hid me so well. I wondered if he knew I was there this entire time. The handsome man closed his left eye as if it was a secret message to me and reopened it a second later. As he left, the people behind him followed in his path. Part of me wanted to trail behind him and ask who he was, but he wouldn't understand me anyway.

When they had cleared completely, I crept up to Annowan, who was giving out the red 'apples' from the wooden basket to the others in our tribe. I looked over toward Aponi's home and saw that her father, Chogan, stood before the door as if to block it. He was clearly protective of his family and had every right. I bet Aponi was behind him, trying to figure out a way to escape the house despite her father's warning. Luckily, the unfamiliar people seemed offer kindness our way. I took one of the 'apples' in my hand and turned it around a few times, checking every part of it out. Finally, I gently bit into it and felt the sweet juices come out of the delicious treat. I wondered where they got these from and if there were more.

"We must be careful," the chief said in a stern tone. "We do not know these people and therefore, cannot trust them. They give us gifts, but it could be a trick. From now on, no one in this tribe can walk alone. Always have another person with you at all times."

"Even I will make sure I am beside one of our tribespeople during this time. Having experienced some of the most terrifying things in this life, trust me and your chief. We do not want you to have to do the same," his brother, Abornazine, firmly said.

The others nodded their heads. Chogan finally walked out from the entrance to his home and Aponi came rushing out as if she was some type of guard dog that had been locked up. She looked all around and met my gaze. When she walked up to me, I already knew exactly what she would say.

"What happened?" she eagerly asked.

"A group of people that I never saw before…maybe another tribe? They gave us gifts. They are…'apples.' I tried one, and it is so delicious…" I trailed off.

"What did they want in return?" she continued with her questions.

"Nothing. We just gave a fur covering to help in the winter that will be coming soon."

"They will want more; I am sure of it," she said. I handed her another apple from the wooden basket and she shook her head, refusing it.

"Aponi, why would they give us delicious treats if they were only going to be mean to us in some way? Besides, the man in the front…" I felt my cheeks grow red and guessed they were likely a similar shade of the apple.

"Oh, no…no no no." Aponi wrapped her arm around my back and guided me toward the pile of clothes that she clearly saw were mine from when I dropped them onto the ground. "You are not getting caught in a tangled web like that."

"He's just so interesting. I don't think I'm going to be able to stop thinking about him the entire night," I said as I picked up some of the clothes. Aponi began piling them on top of my arms.

"You heard our chief. They are off limits to us to even talk to… I can't imagine what Annowan would say if he knew you were developing feelings for one of them…" She took half my pile and we headed towards the stream.

Aponi

9

Agisa reminded me of young love when the mind doesn't work any longer. Any warning signs will quickly be overlooked while you pursue an almost impossible person who may not even be right for you. This was much like when I began to fall for Catori and I was sure that Agisa would end with the same heartbreak as I did. I looked down at my scars and winced as if the pain had come again at that very moment. The physical pain came nowhere close to what I felt in my heart on a daily basis. Even worse, Agisa was falling into a similar trap I had when love took ahold of me. In her case, we didn't even know this strange man…let alone what he was capable of. At least with Catori, I knew I could trust him from when I was just a child. He never had any bad intentions when it came to the people around him. I knew it pained him to hunt…although he was one of the few in our tribe that had the best aim, he would purposefully miss for the sake of the animals' lives. Catori was born a protector of all, whether it came to the animals around us, his family, or even just me.

"Aponi? You okay?" Agisa had been talking the whole time while I just stared off into the distance toward the path that led down to the shores where I could walk to the island. She seemed to meet my gaze and I could tell she knew where my mind was.

"Oh, yeah. I'm fine—" I answered her. This was something I was used to saying by now, even if I wasn't.

"Hey, you helped me with everything the other day. I'll bring them back today so you can rest. You look like you haven't slept in a while," she said, trying to help.

"What a nice compliment from you, Agisa. And you look like you haven't brushed your hair in days!" I snapped right back at her. Sometimes, I wished I could have had a sister so that I could entertain myself with the back and forth silly fights. Agisa just smiled because she knew I was only joking.

"Be careful, okay?" she reminded me.

"Don't go chasing after that man…maybe you're the one who needs to be careful." I smiled back at her. Her cheeks turned a bright shade of red at the mention of him.

"Shh, don't tell anyone!!" she screamed as she piled up the clothes and walked off to go back to the longhouse. "I'm serious, don't!" she called back without turning my way.

"I won't, I won't. Your secret is safe with me," I assured her. As she walked away, I realized we were the only two remaining at the stream. My eyes drifted down the path and I could feel a pull to venture in that direction. A strong wind came and pushed the leaves about on the ground, causing them to form a repetitive dance until they mirrored one another and fell flat to the ground as the wind died down. I hesitated while I looked, but could not seem to ignore what I felt in my chest. It was as if something was pushing me to go down there. After a few more moments of rethinking it, I followed what I felt in my heart and found myself walking down toward the shores. The palms of my hands felt clammy, so I rubbed them against my sides, nervously continuing on. I peeked over my shoulder to make sure no one saw me going out this far. A sudden shift in the wind caused the leaves to whirl about before me. In the distance, I could hear twigs snap as if someone were walking over them. I stopped where I stood and quickly moved to hide. Someone must have spotted me going this way. If it was one of the tribespeople, they would've surely said something. It was likely that it was one of those men that rode the horses. I tried to quiet down my breaths, but felt like it was too late since they likely already saw me. When I heard another twig snap ahead, I hid completely behind a tree and no longer peeked out. This time, it sounded much closer to where I was. My heart pounded in my chest while I wished I had made a run for it when I first heard the noise. How wrong was I to venture out instead of going back to the longhouse with Agisa… With great reluctance, I peeked out one last time…curious what laid before me.

Light brown fur lined the outside of its body. Specks of white were painted over its back, while a thick strip of white covered underneath its darker coat. Giant ears poked out, much too large for its small head. It looked scared beyond belief and was staring straight at me. I had seen fawns before, but usually with their family…never alone.

"Hey, it's ok…" I called out, relieved that it was only a harmless deer. This reminded me much of Catori's encounter with the deer that he rarely spoke of. It stepped backward, but its ears remained alert. I stopped walking toward it and kneeled down so I could appear smaller. "I won't hurt you," I said as I placed my hand out. It stayed where it was and tilted its head to the side, confused. Reaching into my bag, I took out some berries I had found and extended my hand out as to offer them to the fawn.

After a few moments, it began to walk in my direction...still hesitating. Its steps were slow and careful. I thought of how it was probably looking for its mother and was likely lost and scared. As soon as it reached my hand, I could feel the fur tickle my fingers while she sniffed the berries and gently took them in her mouth. She put her head down and I was able to stroke in between her eyes with two of my fingers. When the strong wind blew again, it seemed to alarm the fawn of something. She walked away and peered over her back as if to tell me to follow her.

"You want me to come?" I asked, feeling just as crazy as the tribespeople likely thought I was for doing half of the things I had on the island a year ago. In a silent response, the fawn continued on. As I followed, she peeked back at me like she was making sure that I was still following. We walked all the way down the path that led to the shores and as soon as we came to the end of the woods, the fawn kneeled down while facing the island. Something was telling me to look out there. It must have been high tide, since there was no visible pathway that could lead you there. I walked closer to the edge of the sand and let the waters rise over my feet.

"He's gone," I called back to the small deer. When I turned to look at it again, it was gone. All of this confirmed that I was, in fact, crazy. Maybe there was no deer to even begin with. But somehow, I was led here to this spot…staring out at the forbidden land. An even stronger wind came again, causing me to shiver and wish I were at home under the fur blankets. An even deeper part of me wished it wasn't blankets and instead Catori's arms that warmed me. I stared at the island longingly, despite all the horrors I met while there. I wished I could walk across the pathway and find that Catori was okay and only needed help walking back to the mainland. We could all go back to our lives and be happy. But life wasn't like that. Life had a way of testing you as much as it could and in many ways, this did make you stronger…but there were times when someone was given far too many tests to the point they could no longer see the light. There were just a few rocks that were left of the path that normally revealed in low tide. I walked over to them and stood there, staring out. A giant bush of trees filled the land, and it appeared much smaller than how big it was when I walked all throughout it. I squinted as the sun partly blinded me from being able to see more than just the trees. The sandy shores of the island contrasted with the dense green from within. There was a slight movement from something along the outside. It looked like a man slowly walking the island's boundary…like an animal in a cage, pacing. The man's back was faced toward me, but I could see his long, black hair and tanned skin. When he turned, I had to squint even more to make out who he was…but I could see the red handprints on his chest from the night he became chief. A path that had been washed up with the tide lay between us, stopping me from going any further. He seemed to spot me and came as close as he could go. In that moment, my heart knew exactly who it was...

Agisa

10

Pretending as if everything was okay and nothing had changed was one of the most difficult things I ever had to do. As I walked past the others, rumors of the new people filled the air. Who were they, where did they come from, and what were they doing here? Those unanswered questions swarmed my mind too, but stayed in the back of it as my main focus was on the mystery man who gave us those delicious apples. His light features clashed with every single man I had met, let alone everyone in our tribe. He did not fit in, but that made him all the more beautiful. Aponi didn't seem to agree with me it was possible for me to follow my heart for a man like him, but it seemed odd given her situation. I wasn't always close with Aponi, but had known her my entire life and could tell when she needed time alone. When I left her at the stream, I hadn't even been thinking about the chief's words and warning. No one in the tribe was to walk alone. I hoped she was okay. As I hung the damp clothes on various branches to dry, my mind took me back many years ago to a time when things seemed hard but…looking back now, were much simpler. A time when responsibilities were on the elders and all I had to worry about was following what the chief said.

As children, we would play most of the time and sometimes help with the elders' responsibilities.

Women and men would often go their separate ways once they reached a certain age. I had lived just past seven winters when the spring came. Snow that had once blanketed the grounds around us was now melted as it revealed stalks of grass that poked out from the dirt. Birds sang their songs while they built nests for their young, and trees regained color after the harsh winter. I remember walking behind Mother while she was on her way to work in the garden. Aponi shouted out from the distance and the boys trailed after her as if they were playing some game of chase.

"Why don't you go play with them?" I remember Mother calling back to me. I shrugged my shoulders in response. Back then, I had been shy in front of everyone but Mother and Father.

"I don't know," I said.

"Well, I'm not going to force you…but you should try to play with them. Come on, they will love you!" she insisted. I took a deep breath and shook my head, continuing on with Mother. From then on, I always avoided the others, and that's when I found my passion for painting. When Mother was gardening, I used some remains from the various fruits and flowers to practice with. There was a long slab of cloth that she had given me to try to draw on. Mother also gave me some berries that weren't quite ripe enough yet, but had fallen onto the grounds and were too bitter to eat. I would use a tool to smash it in a bowl, then dip my fingertips into the mixture. On a lighter surface, the colors came out much more vibrant. The greens of the unripe berries brought life to the once blank picture. I added some other things I had found which created darker tones.

Tracing a trunk with its long branches, I made a tree. With my fingertips, I swirled the green around in circles to show its leaves.

"What did you paint, Agi?" Mother said, admiring my work.

"Home, I painted home," I answered, looking at the lone tree that symbolized my home then and still does now. This same painting is now in my family's home.

I smiled, thinking about the daydream that I just had. Thinking about the simpler times sometimes reminded us of the good that still remained in some ways. When I walked into our home, I looked at that painting from what seemed like it was just yesterday. In many ways, I felt like that tree when I was just a child. Although I was alone, I still felt at home with myself. I wished I would've snapped out of it and just gone to play with the others, but there was always something that stopped me from doing so. I knew they were nice and would have accepted me, but I now realize it was me who had to accept the person who I was.

"Agi, what's wrong?" I nearly jumped where I stood. Father came up from behind and startled me.

"Nothing, why?" I answered, trying to take deep breaths to slow down my racing heart.

"You come to look at that painting whenever something is bothering you. What is it?" he asked, knowing me inside and out.

"Who are those people who visited our home?" I asked. This wasn't the main thing that was on my mind, but it was a question I had been meaning to ask him. Father was very close with Annowan and despite him being less social since Catori went away, he was one of the few who remained by his side in hunting.

"They are outsiders...they have come from a different place," he said what I already knew.

"But from where?" I asked.

"We don't know, but we don't think they can be trusted."

"Did you try one of the red apples they gave us?" I asked, trying not to reveal my interest in the man who gave us the delicious gifts.

"Yes, actually. Annowan had a few more, and they were some of the best fruits I had ever feasted on. I was a little bit worried at first about eating it, but when I saw him do the same, it showed me it was safe," he said.

"We should get some more apples...what do you think they would want to trade us for?" I asked, feeling silly for mentioning a negotiation. Father smiled at my remark and messed up my hair with his hand as he patted me on the head.

"I don't think Annowan is worried about getting more apples right now…" Father said.

"So, now what?"

"Annowan has invited them to a feast tonight. It is difficult because we do not speak the same tongue they do…so he is trying to draw a picture of some sort so they will understand," he revealed. I felt a shock in my body as an idea sprung from my mind.

"Father!! Let me draw the picture or paint it. I would love to do that!" I smiled, tugging his arm.

"Well, it needs to be done as soon as possible because the feast will be tonight…"

"Yes, yes! I'll even get it done by midday!" I said, happily hopping about the room to gather supplies. Father stood there laughing as he watched me struggle to grab all the things I thought I needed for this extravagant painting. I would get it done and hand it to Father so he could bring it to the 'outsiders.' And at the feast...I would finally see him again and it would no longer feel like he was part of a dream.

Aponi

11

It took everything in me not to swim out to the island. I knew from last winter how the mind could play tricks on itself...especially when spirits were involved. But I still couldn't seem to ignore what my eyes saw. There was only one person who would possibly understand. I sprinted through the woods and down the pathway that led back to our homes. Passing by our home, I saw Father as I continued walking.

"Hey," he called out to me, stopping me in my tracks despite how difficult it was to do so.

"I have to go see Catori's grandmother," I told him the truth, but wasn't planning to reveal anymore than I had.

"Just make sure you're back in time to prepare for the feast tonight, okay?" he said.

"Feast? We haven't had one with our tribe in so long…what's changed?" I asked.

"We have invited the unknown tribe to show them peace," he admitted.

"Okay, Father." He walked over and kissed me on the forehead, then I went on my way. It was just a little bit longer until I would enter a place I hadn't dared to even look at upon passing in a while. The same deerskin that covered the entrance was still ripped slightly on the bottom from when Catori and I played hide-and-seek while we were just children. I thought back to the time

I had been hiding in his home and when I heard him coming, I tugged on the deerskin as hard as I could so he wasn't able to come in and find me. When the bottom ripped slightly, I became so upset since the guilt swarmed around me.

"It's okay, it was my fault," Catori had said to me.

"But that's not true. I shouldn't have been tugging it in the first place."

"I pulled it at the bottom. It's okay, I'll tell Father I did it," he insisted.

That was one of the many times he had taken the blame for someone else's doings. I never felt right because of it, but he persisted on it being his fault. He would bear the weight of guilt on his shoulders, so no one else had to. His soul had a unique strength to it that was one of a kind.

I pushed the deerskin away to find that Catori's father and mother were not inside, but his grandmother was the only one in the home. She was sitting on his old bed, cutting a new shirt out of deer hide with a knife. His bed remained just as he must have left it, unmade, with his blankets in a pile. He was one to sweat in his sleep since he always pushed them as far as he could toward the end of his bed.

"I haven't seen you in a while," his grandmother said in a low, strained voice without turning my way. She had this way about her where she could tell who entered the room without even looking.

"Haven't seen you either," I said right back to her.

"How do you think this would have looked on him?" She finally turned to face me and held up the long deer hide shirt that could have easily slipped over Catori's head. It looked comfortable to say the least, but would surely come down to my ankles if I wore it.

"On Catori?" I asked. She didn't answer, and I assumed my guess was right. "I think it would look really great on him. It's soft deer hide, and he always liked being comfortable."

"Oh, you know him…if he could, he would bring that fur blanket of his wherever he went," she chuckled under her breath.

"That's what I have come to talk with you about…" I began as she looked over at me. "Something strange happened earlier today."

There was no response as I waited for her to urge me to say more. I wasn't sure how she would perceive this or if she'd just think I was crazy. Looking into her deep brown eyes and seeing the wisdom of many years that showed on her face, I decided to go ahead anyway. I knew she was the first person Catori always went to when it came to anything. She was a safe space. But where would I start?

"I saw him," I blurted out, unable to hold myself back from leading up to exactly how I reached that point. When I ran back to the tribes' homes, it took everything in me not to shout he was still alive.

"Saw who?" she asked at which point I walked over and took her hands in mine, hoping she would believe me...despite how unbelievable a thing this was.

"Catori is still here. I saw him." Saying the words aloud made me that much more hopeful. At the same time, it was a very dangerous game since that hope could be quickly crushed at any moment.

"Did you get enough sleep last night?"

"I'm telling you the truth. I was washing clothes with Agisa and she left...so I was alone. Out of nowhere, a fawn came to me and led me to the shore. From there, I could see Catori standing on the island looking back at me," I persisted.

"You are sure it was him you saw?" Her eyes seemed to glimmer with hope as mine must have, too.

"I promise."

"These spirits sometimes play tricks on us...I want you to be sure of it."

"I know, but what if it is really him that's there, and he is trapped? What if he needs us to help him?" I asked.

"It is full of risk," she reminded me of something I already knew, but didn't care about. If there was even a small sliver of a chance he was alive, I would risk anything to bring him back.

"When the evil spirit took him, I felt in my heart he was still here…I can't ignore what I saw."

"What do you plan to do?" His grandmother pulled her hands out of my grasp and kneeled beside his old bed, pulling out a small bag that had been shoved underneath. I wondered what she was doing, but was just glad to finally be talking about what I saw.

"I need to go there."

She shook her head at me and didn't respond to my idea. But instead, she was fumbling around with the bag she had taken out and reached her hand inside. She pulled out two necklaces that had matching half moons on each side. It looked like they were two pieces that would fit perfectly together. The half moons were white and dangled down from a thin piece of deer hide all the way around. I walked over and she placed one in my hand. She then walked around to my back so she could place the other necklace over my head. She tied it in the back while I looked down at it, wondering where it came from.

"Catori gave these to me before he went to help you. He told me if anything ever happened to him to present these in your time of need..." she said. "I had completely forgotten they were still here until you came."

"He made these?" I asked, feeling a tear stream down my cheek.

"He was going to ask you to be his partner in life. He said that together, you reminded him of the moon when it was fullest in the sky."

"But how will this help me now?" I asked, wiping my tears.

"Catori and you were two peas in one pod. And I knew Catori like the back of my hand…if there was something he had his heart set on, he was going to do anything it took to get it." She lifted her eyebrows as if to point out I was a living example of that.

"You are the same," she continued. "I know that no matter what I say or anyone else says, you will find a way to go there. We would have to tie you down to ensure you never ventured out to the island."

"Well…that is right." Part of me wanted to protest, but I knew what she was saying was, in fact, true…

"There is one piece of the legend that could be true. If the spirit is strong enough…it will fight its way through the evil. Its soul will shine to its full extent in the light of the day. When night creeps up at dusk, that evil spirit will take control again."

"So it is possible that Catori will be there as long as I go during the day? The beast will not be there?" I asked, as my mind raced faster than I could form my words. There was so much more I wanted to question.

"It is unlikely, but if his spirit is strong enough…then, yes."

I started touching my fingertips against Catori's half of the moon I held in my hands. His grandmother wrapped her warm hands around mine, enclosing the necklace in both of our palms.

"Only Catori knows of this necklace. You remind him of who he is and that might just save us all…" A sense of urgency filled her eyes as I stared back into them, feeling as if I carried the entire world on my

shoulders.

Agisa
12

I spent the entire morning attempting to create the drawing so Father could hand it to the chief. It wasn't easy trying to think of how to communicate 'want to come to a feast?' to these people who didn't know our language. When I finally turned it in to Father, his face looked pleased.

"This is perfect, Agi. You drew our tribe on one side of the longhouse and the fair skinned men on the other side. We have some plates of food in our hands. Great job." He patted me on the back a few times.

"Do you think they will be able to tell the time of day that we will be eating together?" I asked.

"The sun in the sky has just met the horizons, so I would say so!" he said. "And if they still don't understand, we can send someone to go gather them closer to when we have the feast."

"Okay, Father. I am going to help the others to prepare," I said.

"Just make sure you do not walk outside our homes alone," he warned. I nodded in response and left to go find Aponi. When I last spoke to her, something wasn't right. She seemed like she needed her space, but I wanted to make sure she was okay. I walked past her home to head for the stream, but decided to turn back; there was a small chance she was inside. When I was just about to go in, I saw her coming out of Catori's home instead. She looked shocked to see me there. Just when I was about to open my mouth to ask what she was doing inside his family's home, she put her arm on my back and guided me in the opposite direction.

"Shhh… don't say anything. We need to talk, but not here," she whispered. The confusion I felt likely spread over my face as we passed by the others in silence. There was so much to do still for the feast tonight, but Aponi was here guiding me away from the work I needed to do.

"You two look like you are up to something fun. Mind if I join?" Mato asked. I just looked over at Aponi because it seemed that it was not entirely up to me. Her urgent expression remained unchanged.

"Just come on," she whispered and continued on. Mato trailed behind us and part of me wished it was just Aponi and I going to talk because I had more to say about the mysterious man that I still could not stop thinking of. We walked toward the stream and she finally stopped.

"You both need to promise not to tell anyone about this. Okay?" she asked.

"About what?" Mato was the first to say.

"Just promise, okay?"

"Okay," I said.

"Sure," Mato finally gave in. With that, Aponi did not respond and just looked all around us as if to make sure no one was coming. Then, she walked down the path that led to somewhere we all were far too familiar with. It was too late to turn back since I was sure Mato's curiosity was piqued just as much as mine…if not more. I peered over at Mato as Aponi led us, and we locked eyes. He had been looking over at me this whole time and I hadn't even noticed. I just shrugged my shoulders as if to silently say 'I don't know' and looked the other way.

"Okay, I am bringing both of you here because I trust you. What you are about to see is something I never thought could actually happen, but I always felt a small sliver of hope in my heart…and I want you guys to help me," she said.

Aponi, asking for help? Was this still the same girl I had known my entire life? Whatever this was must've been of great desperation on her part. As soon as the crashing of the ocean waves filled the air, I could tell we were getting even closer to the shore. What had once been fallen leaves that we pressed down into the ground even further with every step we made, was now soft, bare sand. My feet felt like they were sinking in the farther I walked out. A thick strip of seaweed lined the middle of the sandbar. As we stepped over it, Mato reached the other side first and held his hand out to me. I took it and carefully stepped over the slimy bits of green.

"Thank you," I said as Mato smiled back at me. I could almost feel my heart drop for him, for the moment he found out I had fallen for another man.

Before we could say anything else, Aponi put both hands on her hips and looked back at the two of us as if we were just children and she was about to teach us something.

"Catori is alive," she said. As if Mato and I were sharing thoughts, we exchanged glances and then looked back at her. She had officially lost her mind.

"What do you mean?" I asked.

"He can't be," Mato added.

"I'm telling you. I came here…was led here and saw him on the island." She paced back and forth, clearly frustrated with us. Mato walked to the edge of the shore. His muscular arms crossed over his chest as he peered out at the island. It seemed so far away, but at the same time…we were unable to walk all the way there because the walkway was covered completely in water.

"I don't see him, Aponi," he said.

"Just keep looking. I'm telling you, I saw him!" she persisted.

"And you're sure?" Mato said. Aponi nodded and walked up next to him. I followed closely behind, but kneeled on the sand. I stared at the several shells that lined the shore. The soft sand felt soothing underneath my palms as I gathered a clump in my hands. Tiny specks of sand flowed out while I gradually opened my palms. I remembered something my grandfather had told me when we went to the shores once. 'Each of us in this world is like a grain of sand. It is so much bigger than just us, but we must do our part in order to help life continue on.' As I looked back up at Aponi, I could feel her desperation to have Catori back.

"How?" I questioned.

"How what?" Aponi asked.

"How would he still be here?" I said, worrying she would take my question the wrong way.

"I don't know…well, I didn't, but then that's why I went to go see Catori's grandmother."

She kneeled beside me and Mato still looked out at the island as both of us gathered sand and dropped it again and again.

"What did she say?" I asked.

"There's a chance his spirit is strong enough to fight off the evil. If it is, then the Wendigo can only take over his body by night."

"Okay, if this is true...what do you plan to do?" Mato walked over to us, giving up on looking for Catori from the mainland.

"I need to go there during low tide, but I want you guys to distract the others while I go."

"What?!" I jumped up. "You almost died, and he saved you so you could survive. I don't think he would want you to put yourself in danger yet again."

"I'm sorry, but I agree with her," Mato said.

"I know what you're saying, but I can't just give in to my fears. I need to face them head on and if I don't do this, I will never forgive myself," she explained.

"But then that will mean that all Catori gave was for nothing." Mato reminded her.

"So you're saying if there is even a slight chance of being able to save Catori, I shouldn't take it?" she asked. The twinkle in her eye as a tear formed in the corner made me want to cry for her, too. The way she explained it made me understand why she wanted to risk it.

"Just let us know what you decide and we'll try to help however we can," Mato said. I nodded his way to let him know I agreed.

"Tonight...at the feast. I want you to cover for me somehow. Maybe I wasn't feeling well and couldn't come? Please, just do whatever it takes. Everything depends on this," she begged.

Aponi

13

Choice...it was a tricky thing when given the option. If one chooses to walk away from what they truly want, they will forever think about what could have been if they might have taken the chance. If you imagine two doors, but you only ever take the same plain one that you're used to because you are familiar with it and the unknown frightens you...that's all it will ever be. In order to achieve your dreams, you have to take a risk, no matter how scary it might be. The unknown can bring you to the unimaginable. You'll look to the past and no matter what, be thankful you at least took that chance.

There was no turning back now; no matter how hard I tried…I couldn't unsee him. It was as if a door was opened and I was being pushed through without the choice to turn around. But then again…even if I did have a choice, I wouldn't change a thing. The sun began to fall, casting shadows on the world around us, and I knew my time was running out. Mato and Agisa said they would cover for me if anyone was looking, but I had a feeling everyone would be busy enough with the people they invited for the feast. If there was a good time to go, it would be now, and I had to make sure I was at least home before night fell over the skies above. I felt like the grains of sand that Agisa held in her hands at the shore earlier reflected the time I had left that was quickly running out before I could even begin to grasp it.

My friends left me sitting there on the shores, watching as the tide dropped and revealed the path that slowly but surely emerged. The moments waiting caused me to sweat at my palms despite the cool fall air. I was hoping I would see Catori at least once more to confirm my suspicions, but the shore that lined the island remained empty and bare. I sat there and waited…hoping for some sign to show me that going down the path before me was the right decision to make. As the path revealed more and more, I began walking down its rocky, shell-filled grounds. Several shells broke with each step I took. Thankful for the deerskin boots, my feet wouldn't have survived the walk if I didn't have them. When I reached about halfway down the walkway, I turned around to see that the mainland appeared smaller the farther I walked away from it. My heart pounded in my chest; I was tempted to turn back. What Mato said was true. If something happened to me while on the island, all Catori had given and sacrificed would be for nothing. In the distance, the leaves from a tree rustled faster than the wind had moved them before. The lone deer that had brought me here just this morning came in to view. It walked closer toward the end of the mainland, where the path opened up and kneeled down, staring at me. It was as if she was blocking my way back, telling me to continue on. I glanced at the island again, then back at her.

"I'm so scared," I said, feeling like there was a lump in my throat, stopping me from saying anything more.

She got up slowly from where she stood and walked closer to me until she stood right about arm's length away from me. I felt her soft nose nudge into my side, gently pushing me farther down the path. As I looked back, I felt a great strength grow in me from the slight touch of the fawn. It was the sign I needed to keep going. I walked down the remainder of the path without turning back this time. Making it all the way to the sandy shores, I felt a sense of accomplishment. I never even thought I'd be standing here ever again, yet here I was. The island felt much bigger now while I stood on its grounds. I looked over to the bush where my limp body lay just last winter, almost completely drained of every last breath I had. When I saw my scars again on my arms, it felt that much more real instead of just a bad nightmare.

When I turned back to see the mainland, I was quickly surprised it was now bare of any fawn that I had previously seen. The deer wasn't even back on the mainland as far as I could see. Relentlessly crashing tides of the ocean roared in my mind as they traced up the coast of the island and retreated out once again. It was only a matter of time until the walkway was hidden beneath the waters. I could feel a presence beside me. Its breaths filled the cold air with more condensation than if it were just me standing there alone.

"Aponi?" his voice said. I jumped around to find Catori just as I had once known him, except his body was without any scar or blemish. He appeared to be a human; you couldn't even tell of the beast that lurked within his cursed soul. I couldn't even make any words, but instead, I just wrapped my arms around him in a hug and wished that I was glued to him. In that moment, I feared letting go since there was no knowing whether or not I would ever see him again. The softness of his eyes made it hard to believe he ever did truly become the beast that haunted this island and could creep into the dreams of the most vulnerable minds. He wore the same pants made of deerskin he had originally come here in. Catori's chest was bare and made his body all the more inviting. His warm skin cured the goosebumps that covered my own. As he held me in his arms, I couldn't help but feel like he was pulling back and didn't want to be anywhere near me.

"I'm not strong enough," he said. It reminded me of the dream I had.

"What do you mean?" I asked, still resting my head on his chest.

"I don't want to hurt you. You shouldn't be here." He pulled away from me and my reluctance was no match for his strength.

"I'm already here. You wouldn't hurt me."

"You don't understand, Aponi. If I was so sure of that…I would have tried to see you long ago. I would've come out and waved to you instead of just cowering behind the trees watching you as you stared out at the island all those times."

"So, you've been watching me?" I looked back at the mainland where I would stand every day, gazing out at the island, and thought of how he had been doing the exact same thing this whole time.

"Knowing you were at least okay was all I needed to keep going…even if it meant giving up being with you."

"But you don't need to. You're here," I persisted.

"I can only control it so much…" He kneeled to the ground and placed his head in his hands.

"The fact that you can control it even a little bit means a lot." I stroked my fingers through his thick, black hair. Its tangled mess reminded me of mine when I woke up each morning. "Catori, you are stronger than you think." I kneeled beside him. When I took his chin in my hand, he was looking back up at me again.

"What is this?" he asked, gently grasping his hands around the half-moon necklace I wore. I forgot I even put it on and pulled the matching one from my pocket to hand to him.

"Your grandmother gave me these that she found under your bed. You made these and didn't even tell me?"

"I wanted to give it to you at the right time," he said.

I placed it on his neck and made sure it was tied loosely so that he would still have it, even if the beast took over his body again.

"I can't let anything happen to you again." His eyebrows lifted with worry. I couldn't hold myself back any longer and pressed my lips into his. Right before I closed my eyes, I could see the surprise light up his face. The pounding in my chest overpowered the sound of the waves crashing onto the sandy shores. I felt myself press into him even more, our lips tearing apart only to take quick breaths.

"I've missed you so much." He pulled away, saying exactly what I was thinking. There was no other place I would rather be.

"I thought you were gone forever." I felt the tears as they trickled down my cheeks. They seemed to match everything else I was feeling while the walls I had so carefully put up came crashing down. I was here, finally giving in to everything I felt the more I kissed him. "We need you back on the mainland."

"The curse has to be broken…and you know the only way that happens. The beast must take over another soul."

"What if there's another way?" I asked, thinking about what Catori's grandmother had told me. I sat down next to him and we watched the waves rise again and again.

"Another way?" He looked at me with those sweet, soft eyes that caused my heart to melt.

"Your spirit can break the curse," I said, firmly believing in what I was told.

"I don't know about that…but you need to keep the others away; I fear I won't be able to control myself, especially in the night."

"Have you killed?" I asked.

"Yes," he looked down with regret. "No one that looked like they were from our tribe, but the evil had overcome me and before I knew it, I found myself standing over his body…"

"One of the unknown tribe," I gasped, thinking about the man that Agisa's heart was set on.

"Unknown tribe?" he asked me, confused.

"One day, a whole tribe of men came to our homes on their horses. They had tamed the horses and were using them to get around from place to place. This tribe had much lighter skin than ours and looked like people we had never seen before."

"Oh, no…" he said.

"Like I said…we need you." I tried changing the topic to give him more hope that all wasn't lost. The sunlight had begun to fade into the horizons and I knew the small amount of time we had together was coming to an end.

"You need to go." He got up and held out his hand. I took it and kissed him one last time. A weight sat in my chest since I didn't want to leave, but knew I had to.

"I will come back," I promised. He returned a faint smile that appeared to be a mask on his face for what he truly felt.

When I walked down the path, I thought about the glimmer of hope that my life depended on. Without that bit of faith, I wouldn't have come as far as I did. The rocky path trailed behind me and sand now lined all that stood before me. I looked back, but couldn't see

Catori any longer. Just as the sun had disappeared into

the depths of the horizons, so had he it seemed.

Agisa

14

It takes a lot for someone to make up their mind. But when they are set on a certain thing, one must move mountains in order to get them to forget what their sights are so focused on. Seeing how Aponi was still hopeful that Catori was out there somewhere made me realize the true magic that love was. For love was the one thing in the entire world that could not be bound, but instead…would always, always find a way out. One could only hide it for so long until the truth was revealed to all. And sure, there was a chance. There was a slight chance that Catori was still on the island and could be saved, but was it worth the risk? To Aponi, the answer to that question would be yes over and over again. And I didn't blame her for it.

I regretfully followed Mato as we left Aponi on the shore to go out to the island as soon as low tide came. There was no knowing if we would ever see her again, and the guilt was already eating me up for leaving her there alone. That is what she insisted on, though.

"Don't you think we should head back?" I asked Mato as we walked through the many bare trees that lined the woods on the way back to our homes.

"She won't ever give up, you know her."

"What are we going to tell the others?" I sighed and wished he was wrong, but knew the truth about her stubborn ways.

Mato just shrugged and combed his fingers through the shaggy, dark strands of hair that hung down over his face. I knew he could tell I was worried and didn't know what to do. He stopped walking and turned to me.

"Agisa…I don't know if Aponi told you this, but I have liked you for a long time," he said, looking down at the ground as if he couldn't face me while saying what he said.

"Well, I've liked you too. You're a good friend," I replied, an answer I knew he wasn't looking for. He walked up to me and rested a hand on my shoulder. His coarse palm felt as rough as bark against my skin.

"That's not what I mean." This time, he looked directly into my eyes instead of avoiding eye contact. I was the one who looked down at the ground, not knowing what to say.

"I don't think now is the time for this, Mato. We need to make sure our friend is okay." It was true, but part of me couldn't crush his hopes to be with me by revealing I had my heart set on someone else...who I didn't even know, for that matter...

"You're right. I'm sorry," he apologized and took his hand off my shoulder.

"Listen...we can talk about this later, but for now we need to go to the feast and make sure no one asks any questions about Aponi. Do you know what we should say?" I was the one to put my hand on his shoulder this time. I felt it was comforting to do so.

"Well...we could say she just doesn't feel well, and she's staying in your bed," he said.

"That's an idea. That means we have to get her back before everyone leaves the feast. So, we should take turns keeping watch outside for her to come back the same path that we came from the shores." I made up the plan as I spoke.

"Sounds good to me."

When our homes came into sight, it was surprising to see the horses there, too. Their muscular bodies stood side by side, ready to bring their owners to the next place. They were much different from any wild horses I had seen that roamed freely. It was as though they were imprisoned by their masters in a way. Beside the horses were a few men who belonged to the fair skinned tribe, but not one of them was the man I had been hoping to see.

"I'll be on watch first?" Mato said, breaking me out of my trance.

"Yeah, that works. I'll see you in a bit," I confirmed as I walked past him, eagerly walking into the longhouse to see what awaited. There was a distinct smell from inside and that was the lavender scent that Aponi used to burn whenever we had our feasts. I wondered who started it despite her absence. When I moved the deerskin covering to the side and entered, clusters of people swarmed the center of the wigwam. On one side were the fair skinned men, while the other was full of my people. I walked past each one and they seemed to dress similarly in that they had much more formal clothing, along with shoes that looked nothing like ours. They wore coverings that matched in texture to the rest of their clothes, unlike our fur coverings we wore through the cold. Not one of them flinched as I walked by, seemingly far too amused by whatever they crowded around. I wiggled my way in between everyone to try to get toward the front so I could have a closer look. I felt like turning back and getting out of there to go back in the cold air, since being so close to these people made me sweat worse than in summer. Just as I made my way through most of the crowd and found myself in front, I could see what everyone was looking at.

In the center of the room, two of our tribespeople were dancing around the food that had been cooked for everyone. It was a custom we did, especially at large gatherings. Dancing around meant to celebrate life and each other; it was a way to show thanks to the world and nature around us. Aponi and Catori had done this dance last winter, but this time it was just two others that were a little bit younger than I. They were likely chosen to do this and couldn't reject the offer. I had seen this many times, but was more focused on finding the man that brought the apples. He couldn't have just been a dream. I looked past the tribal dance and saw my father on the other side of the circle cheering them on, along with Mother and Aponi's father and mother. Catori's father stood far back from the crowd beside Abornazine and had the same indifferent look on his face as usual. The men with fair skin clapped as my tribe did their dance in the center, as if to add more music. I thought of Mato and his songs that he could play. They would surely enjoy that. Out of everyone, I still couldn't find the man I was looking for… I turned around and shuffled my way back through the crowds to get to the other side. As soon as I made it, I felt relieved I could breathe again and not feel completely suffocated by everyone. I walked over to the plates of food on the other side of the room and found the red delicious apples that I was longing to have again. I looked back at the crowd and then at the apples again to find someone else's hand was picking one from the bowl too. They held it up and handed it to me. I glanced up and saw him standing there with his arm extended. A gentle smile softened his face; I took it from his hand and didn't know what to say. He wouldn't be able to understand me anyway. I smiled back at him and took a bite out of the apple. My jaws clenched at the juices that poured out as soon as I bit into it. I could tell he knew I liked it because he just laughed as he took an apple too, but didn't have nearly as amusing of a response to its delicious taste.

"Apple," I said as I continued chewing and hoped I said it the correct way in his language.

"Yes." He nodded his head in agreement. I felt very dumb for just saying one word. In fact, I felt like a toddler when they had only learned a few words in their language. Someone who you couldn't keep a conversation with…how would this ever work?

"William," he said the strange word aloud, and when he saw the confused look on my face, he pointed to himself. It must have been his name!

"Agisa," I told him my name and grinned back at him, not knowing what else I could say that he would understand. Just when he put out his hand as if to clasp it around mine to shake it—as he had done with the chief on the first day his people arrived—I had just remembered it was time for me to switch with Mato. I gave William a reluctant wave goodbye and took the rest of the apple with me to go stand outside to relieve Mato of his job. The man smiled again and gave a confused wave, as if he might have asked me why I had to go.

"Took you long enough!" Mato called out on his way past me to go into the longhouse.

"I'm sorry, I got caught up." I could feel my cheeks turn red as I thought of what held me so long.

"Oh, yeah… it sure looks it." He gestured to the remaining half of the apple in my hand.

"They're really good. Try them!" I said and watched as he disappeared into the longhouse. Being outside was a relief, but it was also getting bitterly cold while the sun began its descent in the sky. Smoke formed whenever I breathed out into the cold air as dusk approached. Rubbing my palms together to get warmer, I watched the pathway and hoped Aponi would be back soon. Footsteps sounded behind me, and I spun around to see who was coming my way. It was Aponi's mother.

"Hey, have you seen Aponi anywhere? We're beginning to worry…" she asked.

"Oh, she just didn't feel good. I said that she could lie down at my place," I answered, wondering if it was even believable. The worst thing possible would be for Aponi's mother to suggest going back to check on her daughter in my home, only to find that she wasn't there.

"She's missing out on the big feast?" she asked, confused.

"I guess so…" I didn't know what else to say.

"Do you think I should check on her?"

"Nooo! I mean, no. I think she'll be okay. She just needs some time to rest." I realized how it came off when I said no right away and tried to make it seem less urgent.

"Alright...if you say so. I think I'm going to head back in and if she's still not here in a little bit, I'll go check."

"Okay, no problem," I said.

"Hey Agisa? Thanks for looking out for my girl." She smiled and turned away to follow the same path that Mato had to go into the longhouse. He had likely forgotten about me, just as I had of him while I was in there. I could hear his music, as the people were probably still dancing inside.

"Come on, Aponi...we're all going to be in big trouble if you don't come back in time," I muttered under my breath and continued staring into the dark woods.

Aponi

15

Looking back over my shoulder to see him at least one more time was tempting, but I knew I had to get back before the others found me. Agisa and Mato could only cover for me for so long until the truth came out. As I walked through the woods, night approached and it grew even colder. I shivered and tugged the fur covering closer to my skin. As I approached the tribe's homes, the more distinctly I could hear the melody of Mato's wooden song piece as it hummed out beautiful notes the same as it had long ago on the night Catori became chief. The excitement of Catori and me dancing around the drums made me remember how good it felt to just let go of everything and let loose. The weight upon my shoulders from back then all released as I moved about the room with him. I sighed, wishing I could jump back to that day.

"What took you so long?!" Agisa said, her arms crossed over her chest. She looked annoyed, but also relieved at the same time, if that was even possible.

"I have so much to tell you."

"Well, your mother was just about to go check on you. She thinks you're in my bed resting," she said.

"Thank you for helping me." I couldn't thank her and Mato enough. Without them, I would've surely been found.

"Well, let's go in...we've got to talk about some things."

She looked to be in a rush.

"Oh...the man that you like is in there, huh?"

"William."

"Ah, so a lot has happened for you too! You've learned his name." I smiled as red crept over her face.

"Well, that's about all I was able to learn because we don't speak the same language..." She looked down at the ground. I wrapped my arm around hers and we entered the longhouse together. Everyone was sitting down, eating, while Mato played his calming music. He looked up quickly to see that we came in. As if on cue, his song became even louder.

"There you are!" Mother came running up to me.

"I'm okay now, just needed some rest." I looked over at Agisa to check if the story matched up with hers and she nodded.

"Well, I'm just glad you were able to make it. You should thank your friend Agisa for looking out for you." She gave her a pat on the back. I almost laughed, thinking of how I would often pat a dog on the head for doing a job well done.

"Yeah, she's a good friend," I retorted back. Agisa didn't seem to be paying much attention to our conversation as her eyes darted around the room, looking for that man she talked about.

"Come on," Agisa said, grasping my hand. She pulled me toward the opposite side of the room. When I looked back, Mother just smiled and watched us while we walked away. We came to a table set with several bowls, one of which we stood directly in front of. It was filled with unfamiliar food. Agisa picked one up in her hand and held it up to me. I hesitantly took it from her and just held it, waiting to see what I should do with it. She brought another to her mouth and took a bite out of it.

"This is an apple. It's so delicious, try!" she urged me on. This woman had officially gone mad. But I suppose love could lead you that way… I gave in and took a bite, instantly seeing exactly what she was talking about.

"It's good! Did you find your man?" I asked, knowing full well this was just a distraction.

"No…I did not." She looked around the room behind us again.

"Well, maybe he was tired and went back early!" I tried to cheer her up.

"What was it you had to tell me?" she asked and I couldn't believe I hadn't explained everything to her already. As I looked around us, I made sure no one was close enough to listen. I was glad Mato continued to play his songs, as everyone seemed entranced and occupied by it.

"I saw him!" I smiled, as if I had just found the most magnificent thing ever.

"And?" she impatiently said; I knew she wanted more details.

"He's alive. In the day, he is Catori…when night comes, he is the beast again. We need to figure out a way for the good to win against the evil."

"How do you know?" She asked exactly what I thought she would.

"I first went to Catori's grandmother and told her I saw him. She did say it could be my mind playing tricks on itself, but there's a chance his spirit is strong enough to push the evil back that had taken over his soul."

"So that's why you left as dusk approached?" She was putting the pieces together.

I nodded.

"What are you going to do?"

"I don't know…" I reached in the bowl for another apple and took a bite. Agisa smiled in response as if to say, 'told you they were delicious!'

"I bet you are going to go back there tomorrow …huh?"

"Of course. I'm going to try anyway… There's got to be some way I can remind Catori of all the good so the beast no longer comes out," I said.

"You've got to remind him of who he is."

"You're right. But then there was one more thing. He has killed one of the fair skinned. I don't know who it was, but he was sure it was someone that doesn't belong to our tribe. He said he had never seen them before. You did see your man tonight, right?"

"Yes, I saw William. But this isn't good. If they find out one of their own is dead, they may come after us." Her eyebrows creased together in worry. I felt a weight of relief that it wasn't William who he had taken, at least for Agisa's sake. If they found that there was a beast that lurked the island, they may very well try to fight it. His life was still in danger because the fair skinned stood no chance when it came to the Wendigo that overcame Catori's soul by night. Our own tribe barely survived as it was.

"They might even go after Catori…and if they do that, they are all surely going to be dead."

"I have to warn William somehow before it's too late! I don't know how though because I can't speak his language. Aponi, what should I do?" She was desperate to save the man her heart had fallen for.

"If we find a way to rid the evil spirit from Catori, then we won't need to worry about any of this."

"We've got to do this before it's too late," she said.

"I know."

We walked closer into the crowd of people and took a seat in the back. Despite everyone's enjoyment around us, we both knew that our minds were the furthest they could be from what was going on in that moment.

Agisa

16

The night had come and gone, but all I could do was lay there in bed tossing and turning. Thoughts of how it would feel to run my fingers through his hair kept me up through the night. His bright smile as he flashed his perfectly white teeth at me kept filtering through my mind. While the fire kindled in the center of the room last night, it reflected off his eyes and made them appear to glow when I looked into them. I kept breaking my eye contact with him and looking back at the apples at the feast. I was nervous that my own eyes would remain glued to the beautiful sight of his if I stared for too long. I felt like I had only closed my eyes briefly when the sunlight trickled in from the doorway. Although it was dawn's first light, I felt like the longer I lay there in bed, the more restless I would become. Tip-toeing about the room, I could hear Father's snores and Mother's gentle breaths while they both were sound asleep. I smiled and removed the covering from the door to leave. The faint sounds of a few birds chirping filled the air, but no one stood outside their homes. Everyone seemed fast asleep, for the most part. I gathered a small bag of smashed fruits, tree bark, and small pieces of deerskin that I would often use for my paintings, then headed down the path toward the shore. It was there that I would get most of my inspiration and could listen to the calm of the ocean as I painted.

Passing by the tall trees made me not feel so alone in the way that they were here too…suffering through winter's harsh ways, but would come back again despite all that they went through. I could paint the trees, but they were most beautiful in fall when their many colors were vibrant and different. When I drew closer to the shore, I felt the soft sand under my feet sink down with each step I took. I went farther out and could tell that the tide was receding and Aponi would've likely wanted to be here when it went down all the way. Walking along the shore on the mainland, I focused on the waters as they glimmered in the sunlight's reflection. It reminded me of William's soft eyes that I could get lost in if I stared too long.

A rock with a flat surface was perfect for painting on as I pressed a piece of deerskin down onto it. Using my pestle, I mashed down some sunflower seeds to create a blue tone and added some flowers to the mix. As I stroked my finger through the mixture I made, I gently brushed it against the soft deerskin.

When I was so immersed in painting, I felt a cold tap on my shoulder and nearly jumped out of my skin. I turned to find William standing there with a bag over his shoulder. His hair was messy, and he had dark circles under his eyes as if he hadn't slept in a while. I couldn't have been more confused and wanted to ask him what he was doing there if I could. But all I could say was his name.

"William." I tried to calm my racing heart. He held one finger up as if to tell me to hold on and opened up his bag. He brought out long pieces of wood that resembled thicker sticks with darkened brushes at each end. Some were thinner than the others. While he set them on the rock beside my painting in progress, he brought out small tubes that displayed a different color on each. William placed those beside the other things he brought out. The last thing was a flat, wooden board. Taking one of the small tubes that had a light blue color displayed on it, he squeezed the tube onto the board that he held and grabbed a brush. As he gently pushed the brush into the color, he grabbed a cup of water and slightly dipped the brush in, adding light blue seas to my painting. Before, it wasn't even close to capturing the color of the sea. With his paint, it seemed to bring it new life that it had been lacking. I felt my hand cover my mouth in awe as I watched him add more colors, such as the yellow of the sun in the sky, when it crept up from the horizons. He used color from a black tube with the finest brush to paint small bird-like creatures in the sky. Then he went back and added white, puffy clouds. Below the blue sea, he painted on a very light beige to show the sand that we stood on at this moment. When he picked up the brush he had used for the white, he gently tapped it on each part of the sea to show how it glimmered when the sun reflected off of it.

He looked up at me, seemingly finished with his art. It took everything in me not to lean in to press my lips against his. The fact he shared the same interest as me in painting meant so much and made me feel that much less alone in this world. I felt like I had a lot to learn from him and wondered how he became so good at painting. I took a small brush and dipped it into the black that was on his board. He smiled in response and the amusement in his face was evident as his eyebrows lifted.

On the sand, I made the outline of two people. I added long hair to one and her arms reached up to the man next to her. The man looked down and their faces both touched. I had a feeling he knew exactly what I meant to draw when he placed the board of colors down and reached his hand out to me. I took it in my own and glanced up at him, all sounds completely blocked out and it was just him and I that stood there. I touched my hand to his face and felt his soft skin as he smiled and reached his other hand to grasp mine. In a few moments, he began to speak a few words in my native   tongue.

"It is nice to meet," he said, clearly not fully fluent in my language. It was a good try though, and I could tell what he meant to say.

"William, it is nice to meet you…too." I smiled, thankful we could exchange some words even though they were few. "That is beautiful." I gestured towards the painting.

"Beautiful." he pointed to me. I could feel my face turn red as I held my hands up to my cheeks in embarrassment and smiled.

I turned to completely face him and put both my hands up in front of me; he pressed his palms into mine. The length of his fingers extended much higher than mine and I felt like I had the hands of a child compared to his. His fingers closed down over my hands and the waves came up and down as I allowed myself to get lost in his eyes.

"I like you," I said in my language, hoping that he would understand. He held my chin in his hand and pointed to the part of the painting that I had added where the two people were kissing, then pressed his lips into mine. I almost felt my body lose balance as I had to steady myself by holding on to his shoulder. I could feel his smile press into my own as we continued kissing one another. His chapped lips from the dry air met mine. I reached up to press my hand against the back of his head to push him into me more. Even though we were kissing, it still wasn't close enough. My heart pounded against the waves of the sea that relentlessly came in against the shore again and again. He took my other hand and pressed it to his chest; I felt his heart pound almost in the same rhythm as mine.

"Agisa?" I heard my name being called out. It was Aponi's voice. William brought me to hide behind the boulder and we both laughed like we were just children hiding from our mothers and fathers.

"Bye, Agisa…" William whispered as he kissed me on the cheek. He pointed to the sun in the painting and then pointed to the horizons. "Tomorrow." He promised to see me again at dawn tomorrow and wandered off into the bushes. I stayed there for a few more moments before letting Aponi know I was there. I watched him as he left and wished I could follow him through the woods and we could be alone. The next time that we would meet couldn't come soon enough.

Aponi

17

Just as I was heading down the path to the island, I heard voices coming from behind the boulder. I hoped it was Agisa and called out to her. There was no response. I looked out at the waters and saw that low tide had come just in time for me to cross to see Catori again.

"Right here!" Agisa came out from behind the boulder.

"What were you doing over there?!" I asked and before she could even answer, I could tell exactly what she had been doing just from the look on her face. "So, he met up with you, huh?"

"He is so wonderful…he paints! Today, he brought me a paint set, and it's nothing like I had ever seen before," she could've trailed on, but I began walking toward the pathway.

"Be careful," I warned.

"What do you mean *I* should be careful? Look at what *you're* doing, about to cross over to the island when there's a beast that lurks on it!" she shouted almost too loud for my ears. I looked over my shoulder to make sure no one was watching.

"Stop, people are going to hear."

"So what?! You know, you're not the only one who can find love and have a happy ending…" she was furious, and I had no idea why.

"Why are you saying this all of a sudden?" I asked.

"Ever since we were young, everyone was always so focused on you while I was off on the side pretending as if I didn't exist," she began to walk away and I felt like I had just been stabbed in the chest by someone I had confided in. I sank down to my knees.

"You don't understand. I would give anything to be you. We cannot help who we love, but at least you can be with the one you love. So what good is it to be in my position where I have to sneak out and hope that I come back alive each time?" I pressed my face into my hands while I wished I could tear my hair out and take out every ounce of what I felt on myself instead of the world around me.

"Aponi, I didn't mean..." she began to say.

"I never asked to lose Catori to this beast. Yet, I am the reason he became one…all to save me. What good is saving my life if I cannot even live it with the one I love? I feel I am of great burden on everyone and I have never truly fit in…" I couldn't help it. I sobbed into my hands, wiping the strands of hair away as they clung to the sides of my wet face.

Agisa kneeled before me and picked up my face in her hands, a sympathetic look in her eyes.

"I'm sorry about what I said. I think we are all feeling very stressed right now." She rubbed my back with her hand in circular motions.

"I should just accept that I will never get him back," I sniffled and attempted to stifle back more tears.

"No…never give up. You knew in your heart he was still out there and that there was a chance and look at where we are now. He's counting on you," she reminded me.

"What if I let him and everyone down yet again?" I asked, feeling fully exposed as the wall I had up for far too long had finally come down.

"Then at least you can say you tried." She stood up and held her hand out to me. I took it as she helped me up.

"Thank you," I said and continued wiping my tears.

"You are like a sister to me…and what are sisters for?" She smiled and gave me a hug. "Now, go on out there! I'll cover for you, but don't get stranded when the high tide comes in!"

I walked down the path and looked back to see that Agisa was still there waving at me. When I turned the other way, I was met by the startling gaze of the

Wendigo despite the broad daylight. Its haunting dark eyes glared down at me and, although I felt I was safe, it began to charge toward me on the path. Its monstrous fangs gaped out of its mouth, saliva dripping as it ran. Snarls came from its wolflike snout, but it stood upright like a human would.

"Catori!" I screamed as he came closer. And just as he neared closer to me and I felt like he was going to sink his claws into my flesh like he had last winter....Agisa jumped in front of me to bear the pain. She pushed me out of the way and all I could do was lay on my back, watching as the beast nearly devoured my friend. I finally got a grip on myself and ran toward him.

"Catori! It's me, Aponi!! Get off of her! You're going to kill her!" I screamed at the top of my lungs. The

Wendigo stopped cold and shrank down, its fangs receding and body changing back into a human…the human I had grown to love despite any of his faults. He stood up tall and looked down at Agisa's almost lifeless body as it lay in a bloody mess, claw marks up and down her arms. She lay there panting, trying to gasp for any breath she could.

"What have I done?" Catori asked, looking down at his bloody hands.

"Catori, you stopped it just when it was about to take her," I walked toward him.

"No…no…stay away from me," he said as he stepped back, still assessing Agisa. "You need to all stay away from me. I am a monster."

I shook my head and refused to believe that all he was was a monster. He was more than that and he could win against the evil. Before I could say anymore, he ran back toward the island and disappeared from sight. I kneeled beside Agisa and took off my fur covering so I could comfort her.

"It's okay, Agisa… It's going to be okay. I'm going to bring you back and you'll be okay," I assured her, not fully knowing if she would survive this.

"It's not…your…fault," she grunted through shallow breaths.

"Shh, save your energy. We'll get you back home, okay?" I put two fingers to her lips and got behind her, trying to pick her up the best I could. She was a little bit taller than I, and I had never carried someone of my size before. Every step with her in my arms, I felt like I was going to fall over. The rocky path beneath my feet didn't help matters, as they seemed to dig into the soles of my boots. Just as I reached the mainland, I heard a horse from the distance as its gallops drew closer. A man with light hair and fair skin jumped off the horse as soon as he reached us. He put out his hands and silently offered to take Agisa from me. I was hesitant, as I didn't know this man and wasn't willing to trust a stranger. He insisted, putting his hands out again. Agisa's eyes opened partially as she seemed to recognize him.

"Will..iam…" she whispered. I let him pick her body up much more effortlessly than I had and put her on the back of his horse. He touched his hand to his heart as if to show she meant something to him and rode off into the forest.

It was then that the walls broke down, and I fell to the ground, crying. Just when I had thought I caused enough problems, there I was…creating even more.

Agisa jumped in front of me and sacrificed herself just as Catori had. Why was everyone sacrificing themselves for my sake?

"Aponi?" Mato called out from the forest as he walked closer to me. "What happened??"

"Mato…I don't know. Agisa is very hurt," I said.

"What? Where is she now?"

"One of the fair skinned took her. I couldn't carry her any longer. I am hoping he is taking her back to our tribe's homes."

"How did she get hurt?" he asked.

"The Wendigo got her…" I looked back at the island regretfully and gulped, remembering how painful the claws had been when I was its victim.

Agisa

18

Smooth blue seas kissed the land and gently receded back to their home again into the ocean. The sunlight trickled off the surface, causing the deep blue to shine as if it were magical. This light faded in and out as I struggled to breathe. I suddenly felt the pain wash over me like a tidal wave angrily crashing into me again and again as I couldn't move out of its way and instead felt every bit of it. At one point, I felt like I was dreaming, but then came out of the dream to feel the pain once more.

"Agisa." The desperation in his voice made me want to jump up and let him know I was okay…only I wasn't and could barely stay awake for long enough to notice I was still there beside him. The smooth blue seas that took over my mind were, in fact, William's eyes. When my head fell to the side, I could see we were in the longhouse. Just a few moments ago, I was on the shore with Aponi… I was wondering how I got here so fast. Father kneeled beside me and was no longer that strong, fierce man I always knew him as. Instead, there he was, cowering down to the ground beside me with tears coming from his eyes.

"Please help her," Father said, and I realized William was still standing over me, too. I looked down at my arms and could see the blood as it poured out. William had pushed his sleeves up, but they were still stained red while he wrapped various pieces of cloths around my arms. With each touch, I winced in pain and struggled to lie still. Father reached over and held my hand as he continued to kneel beside me, rubbing the back of my head with his other hand.

"Who did this?" Annowan, the chief of our tribe, asked, although I had a feeling he knew exactly who it was that ripped through me. Thinking about the beast's snarling fangs and monstrous body made me wonder how I was still breathing at all.

"Catori," Abornazine walked out from behind the chief.

"No," was all I could muster up enough strength to say. It wasn't Catori that did this. It was the evil spirit that lurked within his soul, and he couldn't control it. I didn't want them to blame him for what happened to me. Aponi and I should have listened when we were told to stay away from the forbidden land, but there we were walking right toward it.

"My son?" His voice broke when he tried to confirm his suspicions.

"No," I said again.

"Then who?" All eyes in the room stared right at me. I wondered where Aponi went after William must've taken me back to the tribe.

"The beast," I replied.

"She's right. It wasn't Catori; he wouldn't have done this. It was the Wendigo," Abornazine confirmed.

"We need to take away the path to the island," Annowan said.

"You think Agisa was going to the island?" Father asked Annowan.

"Yes, but even if she wasn't on the path…as long as it remains, evil has a direct way to the mainland and to us. I will not let my son die for nothing," Annowan said. I tried to sit up, but fell back down on my back and groaned in pain. William took my hand and rested his arm behind me, allowing me to lean on him as I sat up.

"You can't do that," I said. They all looked at me, confused, wondering how I was standing up for a beast that had nearly killed me.

"Catori is still there," Aponi walked into the room with Mato by her side. He looked at William and then back at me with a defeated look on his face.

"And how would you know?" Annowan crossed his arms.

"I met him," she explained. "By day, he is strong enough to remain human…but in the night, the evil takes over."

"So then, what happened today?" Father asked her as Annowan was clearly processing what she had just said and the fact that his son might still be out there.

"I walked out there to see Catori and make a plan to rid him of the evil spirit, but it was already there…by the time I walked down the path, he was no longer Catori and instead, the Wendigo beast," she admitted.

"So, how does my daughter have anything to do with this?" Father continued to question her. Aponi came closer to me and rested one hand on my forehead, wincing at the sight of my wounds that had already seeped through the cloths that William had tied around them.

"Agisa was painting and saw me go there. She must've seen that he was the Wendigo before I did, and before she could warn me, he was already charging my way. She pushed me to the side and let the Wendigo come at her instead of me..." Aponi said it exactly how it happened. And everything after the moment that the beast launched itself on top of me, I blocked out.

"Is that true?" Father turned to me.

"Yes."

"What do we do now?" Father questioned Annowan.

"Beast..." William blurted out, as he must've understood a bit of what we were talking about. His once soft blue eyes were now a dark, musty color as his eyebrows furrowed down. He held up a long dagger and tucked it away in his pocket again. In the next moment, I felt William's soft lips as they brushed against my forehead and he stomped out of the longhouse in a rage. The sound of his horse's hooves clicking on the ground trailed off in the distance.

"We need all the men we can get right now. I know revenge when I see it and that man will not stop until either he or Catori is dead," Annowan urged the tribe. Father squeezed my hand and went off with the others as they called out to everyone to grab all the arrows, knives and tools they could possibly gather for the impending fight that no one would likely win. Aponi came closer to me and took my hand in hers.

"I'm so sorry," she said, kneeling down. I lay on my back still, but wanted to sit back up and help the others. I felt useless lying here.

"Aponi," I said, and she looked right at me. "You need to go warn Catori. Give it one last try to help him remember who he is. When he was the beast, you were able to break him out of that fate. I bet you can do it again."

"But I've only caused more trouble by doing all of this," she looked down.

"No...it was going to happen sooner or later to someone. Go, before it's too late," I begged and hoped that there would be some good outcome from everything. I wondered what William was doing and hoped it wasn't too late and he wasn't already on the island with his dagger, attempting to face the Wendigo on his own.

19

Good and evil have been two entirely separate things my entire life...or at least, I was taught that way. It was always so black and white without any gray area in between. But then life happened...where the two actually mixed together quite frequently. What is truly good and evil if not what a person makes up in their own mind? When does someone truly turn bad and at that point, is there no turning back?

I ran home to grab my bow and arrow just in case I needed it. When I entered, Mother was with Catori's grandmother sitting beside my bed. It was as if they were waiting for me.

"I know everything," Mother said as she glanced over at Catori's grandmother, then back at me. "You have been keeping this a secret all this time..."

"Mother, I am sorry, but I really can't do this right now..." I walked past them and slung the bag of arrows over my shoulder.

"We know you are going to go no matter what...but just remember what Catori gave for you," his grandmother said. I turned back and saw her standing there across from me.

"I'm his only hope right now," I revealed.

"Or is it that he is your only hope?" Mother asked. "You have been different ever since he sacrificed himself, and this is your only way of making things right."

"It doesn't matter what the reason is…I just need to go," I walked by both of them and was just about to head out of the door when Catori's grandmother stopped me.

"Wait," she said. "You must remind him of his name. Catori means spirit. There are good and bad, but the good always win…they always win in the end."

I looked down at my half moon necklace and rubbed my fingertips against it as she gently touched it with her hands.

"On the day before the full moon…that is when the change can happen. Remember that," she revealed one last thought.

"It will be a full moon tonight," I said, puzzled. She reached her arms out and wrapped them around me, pulling me in for a hug. Mother walked over and hugged me as if it was going to be the last time she saw me.

"I will be back," I assured her, hoping it was of some comfort. Deep down, I was unsure if I really would see her again. The longer I stayed in her embrace, the more difficult it would be to leave. I let go, and she kissed me on the cheek before saying goodbye. As soon as I made it outside, I began running as fast as I could toward the shores. This time, I didn't have to care who saw me because it was very likely everyone was already headed there or still gathering weapons to go after this 'beast.' The soles of my boots were worn out from walking on the rocky path so often. I winced when a few of the rocks' sharp edges poked through to my bare skin. The shores of the island were empty, but I continued running as fast as I could so I would make it before anyone else. I didn't have much of a plan, but just wanted Catori to come out of this alive, no matter what it meant. As I neared the end of the pathway, I breathed a sigh of relief that I made it before the others. I had to warn Catori before it was too late.

The trees swayed back and forth in the wind and towered over me despite being bare of most of their leaves. I walked around the sides of the island looking for Catori, but saw no sign of him. When I came around from the other side, the mainland was in view once again. I could see two very different groups of people coming from a few directions. The tribe, led by Annowan, had tools they were clearly hoping to use to remove the pathway to the island by picking up some of its soil and throwing it out to sea. That way, there would be no walkway any longer. On the other side was a group of William's men led by him as he guided his horse down the path.

Since I wasn't able to find Catori on the outside of the island, I hoped I would have better luck searching for him through the center. I held my bow close to me and placed an arrow in it, ready for whatever came my way. There weren't clear trails within the center, but I was able to find my way around a few trees. Rain began trickling down from the sky as I pulled my fur covering closer to me for warmth. As the raindrops moistened the grounds, it became muddy, and I had to hold on to each tree for balance. A new sound of someone running filled my ears, and I stopped right where I stood. I turned and saw the Wendigo as it ran straight toward me. In a quick attempt to defend myself, I pulled back the arrow in my bow. It flew straight into the beast's shoulder, ensuring the impact wouldn't kill it but only slow it down. The Wendigo was sent back as if surprised by the sudden blow to its body, but continued toward me. I placed another arrow in the bow, but it was too late since I felt my legs fall from beneath me. The wind was knocked out of me while I struggled to catch my breath and realized the beast was on all fours as it snarled over me. Its gaping mouth revealing its teeth as they dripped warm saliva down onto my body.

"Catori," I barely was able to muster up enough strength to say his name. Looking directly into the beast's eyes, I couldn't find even the slightest resemblance to Catori, which scared me all the more. If the evil spirit won, then I was done for…

It sank its teeth into my neck as I moaned out in pain. I extended my arm and reached out for any kind of weapon I could use to defend myself, but saw that my bow and arrow had gone flying in the other direction. The beast pulled its head up and licked its bloody teeth…full of my blood. I reached for the only thing that I could and grasped his necklace as it dangled down over me, surprisingly staying around his neck even as a beast. I pulled it as close as I could until it touched my half of the necklace and when they both met; they created a full moon.

"Spirit," I reminded him, still gasping for air. The beast's eyes changed to a light brown shade. "You have a good spirit," I screamed out. In the next second, a bright light flashed. Standing over me was Catori, with an arrow poking out of his shoulder. As soon as the light vanished, I could see the beast scamper away from us. The entire weight of Catori's body fell down onto me. A stream of blood soaked the fur covering I had been wearing. I brought my hand up to my neck and felt the puncture wounds from the beast's fangs, wincing from the pain I still felt.

"BEAST! BEAST! BEAST!" men shouted from the distance. Catori flinched and picked up his head as he stared down at me. His warm brown eyes showed me the good that I knew he still had in him.

"Aponi..." he said as he continued staring down at me. I pressed my hand into the back of his head, pushing his face into mine. His lips into mine. As we kissed, the group roared on and their voices drifted even closer. But in that moment, we didn't care. It was just him and I. Through all the pain, I quickly pushed any worries away and continued kissing him passionately, knowing that we won. My fingers stroked through his messy, black hair as I turned him gently onto his side.

"Aponi, I love you…" he whispered.

"I love you," I whispered back to him and cupped my palm over his mouth, ripping the part of the arrow that had been poking out of his shoulder still. He moaned into my hand in pain and I urged him to be quiet so the others didn't hear. Catori looked at the wounds on my neck and I felt like he was going to cry with how his face turned pale and sunken. Before I could explain anything to him, the crowds of men drew closer and through the branches, I could see thick sticks with flames atop each of them. Some of the other men carried the longest daggers I had ever seen, as if they meant to stab the beast through its heart.

"Shh," I placed a finger over Catori's lips and we both crouched down as we walked behind some thicker bushes to hide. I shivered from the cold and instantly felt his warm arms wrap around me. As I turned into him, I kissed him again. He moved his lips down to my neck and kissed the two spots where the beast's fangs had punctured. His lips were red with blood and looked even more like the Wendigo that the men were searching for. I licked the back of my hand and wiped his mouth, pressing my lips into his once more.

The flames drew closer, and I stayed there with Catori, hiding him from the others. I could feel him start to shiver from the rain and I untied my fur covering so that I could wrap it around both of us. Before I could do so, I felt his lips on my chest as he passionately kissed every part of my body. I pressed him into me and pressed my lips into his neck, stifling my moans. We stayed hidden behind the bush and quieted one another with our lips so we wouldn't be found. The sounds in the distance faded into nothing as we made love, finally giving in to days and days of not knowing if we ever would again. The passion I felt in his presence overwhelmed my entire body as I leaned my head back in pleasure. He kissed my neck and was gentle with each touch. In that moment, I felt the spirit within me heal every scar I had inside until I felt I could finally live again.

Agisa

20

Lying there while Catori's grandmother kept watch and made sure I didn't wander anywhere made me feel bound to the bed that I lay on. Not knowing who was going to make it out alive was even worse when you had no part in at least helping.

"I need to go there," I complained, barely sitting up.

"And do what? Crawl around? I don't think so…" his grandmother said, continuing to weave thin pieces of deer hide together to make a shirt. "Catori's going to need a shirt when he comes back."

"And how do you know he'll be okay?" I asked. Something about grandmothers always knowing things before they actually happened…

"Just a feeling." She smiled as I groaned while trying to stand up. I fell back to the bed and clenched my jaws in frustration.

"Don't think you're going anywhere…" she said as the once quiet room suddenly filled with noise. The men of our tribe stomped in and walked right up to me.

"Still here," I said, showing that I couldn't have caused any trouble. Annowan came before me and crossed his arms, looking over at his mother and then back at me.

"Where's Aponi?" he asked. I looked to the right and left for the closest escape, but was quick to remember the shape my body was currently in. "Where is she?" he repeated himself, getting closer to me.

"She went after Catori," I gave in.

As soon as I replied, I could hear the same horses from before trotting beside the longhouse. The men with fair skin were all holding something that they carried into the center of the room. With one last heave, they let go at the same time, and the monstrous beast that gave me the wounds on my arms fell flat to the ground. I flinched at the sight of it and worried that the beast could still be alive. Catori's grandmother dropped the shirt she had been making and nearly fell to the floor if it weren't for Annowan's hand balancing her again. If the beast was dead, then that meant Catori was also gone. My heart ached for Aponi and Catori's family as they saw what used to be their loved one, lifeless on the ground. William walked around the beast's body triumphantly and smiled at me. I did not smile back.

Just when I thought Annowan was going to charge toward William, the room went completely silent again. Aponi walked in with her hand held to her neck, but she wasn't the only one who entered the longhouse. Behind her was Catori. While Annowan was busy looking down at the ground, his head rose slightly and there was a complete change in the air. The chief ran over to his son and wrapped his arms around him as he groaned in pain. Both of them laughed when Catori pointed to his shoulder, then to Aponi.

"She is a woman after my heart," he said. "She nearly put an arrow through it."

"And you were about to rip my head off if I didn't," Aponi played back. Across the room, I saw William just standing there, confused. I gestured him to come over to me and with a few quick steps, he was there by my side. I reached for his hand and squeezed it as he helped me to sit up all the way. Aponi walked over to me and Catori came to my side as well.

"Agisa… Aponi and I are forever at your service. You showed the same heroism a chief would for his tribe. Thank you. Because of you, we can be together." He looked over at Aponi and smiled. "And with your help, the curse has been broken."

"Oh yes, let's give all the thanks to Agisa," Mato joked as he walked up to us.

"Mato has been a great help, as well. He has always been!" Aponi patted him on the back.

"Aponi is a stubborn girl and wouldn't let me or anyone else believe you were truly gone," I said as they smiled at one another.

"Anything you ever need...we are here," Aponi assured Mato and me. When I looked over at Mato, I could see he had his arm around the girl had been dancing at the feast the night before. It helped me to not feel as guilty for turning him down. We exchanged a friendly smile to one another and I no longer felt like I had to hide my feelings from anyone anymore.

"This is William." I felt like I should introduce him formally. William held out his hand and at first, Catori just looked at him like Annowan had. But then he took his hand and shook it.

"Nice to meet you," Catori said. Aponi smiled, knowing full well William likely didn't know what he even meant. We exchanged a silly look at one another.

"Eh-'em," Catori's grandmother cleared her throat from behind all of us. He turned around and held his arms out, pulling her in for the biggest hug I saw. His mother walked up from behind and smiled next to Annowan.

"You were going to forget to say hello to your grandmother?" she asked in a sassy tone.

"Of course not. In fact, I only came back here to see you. You know that," he said with a chuckle.

"So, I see you brought me a nice big dinner for tonight." She gestured over to the beast that lay on the floor.

"Come on!! That would be disgusting." He held out his hands as if to say, 'are you serious?!'

I smiled over at William, and he scooped me up in his arms, walking outside with me. I could hear Catori's family laughing in the distance and it was a sound I thought I would never hear ever again.

William effortlessly carried me as if I was a feather in his arms. Dusk fell rapidly, but it felt good to be outside. He gently put me down and held my hand to help me balance. With one gentle kiss on top of my hand, I smiled…returning the favor by reaching up to kiss him on the cheek.

"Agisa…paint with me tomorrow?" he asked in my language. I felt he prepared fully for this conversation and remembered that was our original plan this morning…to meet again the following day. The simplicity in how we could just easily pick up where we left off made my heart feel warm inside.

"Yes, I would like that very much."

Aponi

21

The soul comes into being in this world from an unknown source that we have talked about for many, many winters. Even our elders have discussed how the first person became and what breathed life to the beauty that nature was. One can speculate all that you are is passed down from those that brought you into this world. Others have found glimmers of truth about existence just by looking at the world around us. If you stop and take in the nature that you see, you will find incredible reflections of that upon who you are.

Nature has a way of repeating itself and in that...it always, always balances. The bad in this world must always neutralize with the good and if you think you have seen too much bad in your life, the good is surely on its way.

As the sun rose on the horizon, I knew I had finally found my place in the world. Just as I normally would in the mornings, I crouched down and crept slowly through the forest of trees. Ahead of me was an animal that scurried about. When I looked down at the ground and traced my eyes along the trees and grass that had just begun poking out in time for spring...I couldn't place where the sound had come from and turned back to see that Catori was in the same spot he had just been in, right behind me with his bow...ready to aim. He seemed to hear exactly what I heard, too. I signaled my hand his way to continue walking farther down the path to the shore. In a sudden movement, the animal ran out from behind a tree and I put my hand up as if to say 'stop!' Just as Catori drew his bow back and was ready to release it, I was able to stop him. The scared creature froze before us with nowhere to turn and just stared with its black eyes. As soon as I got a closer look, I could tell it was the fawn from winter's start. It was now beginning to grow its own antlers, but was still small in size.

"This was the deer that led me to you," I whispered back to Catori. The deer's tense body seemed to relax when Catori and I put our arrows back in our bags and tucked the bows away.

"Spirits live on in many different ways. I believe this was a good spirit guiding you to help save me," he said as he crept toward the deer slowly. It didn't flinch, but instead shortened the space that Catori had to walk. It put its head down in front of him and allowed Catori to stroke in between its eyes.

"Come," Catori gestured for me to walk closer to both of them. He took my hand in his and gently guided my fingers against the deer's snout. When I pet its soft brown fur, it seemed to enjoy it and came even closer to me, nudging into my stomach slightly.

"I think he likes me," I said, laughing. It nearly stumbled into me in her attempt to get even closer.

"What is not to like?" Catori asked, leaning over the deer to kiss me.

"Hmm…quite a lot, actually!"

At this, Catori didn't even have to answer. The deer seemed unhappy with my response and nudged me on the side. It jumped back in surprise as I held my stomach. This time, it walked up even more slowly and sniffed where my hand was holding. All of a sudden, I felt pain, and the realization hit me as to why I hadn't been feeling right since the beginning of winter.

"Catori…I think our deer friend has just shown us what will be in our future." I smiled and looked down at my stomach. He looked over at the animal and then back at me, dropping his bow and bag of arrows to the ground.

"What do you think it is??" he asked, clearly not realizing what the deer had pointed out. I grinned at him and tried to find the words.

"Think about what we may have done at the end of fall," I tried to remind him.

"Saved our tribe?" he asked, dumbfounded.

"No, you silly man!" I laughed and pushed him away from me playfully. I pointed to my stomach and then back at him.

"What?!" he shouted, scaring the birds out of the trees above us. They flew away in packs, and I couldn't help but chuckle even more.

"Do you get it now?" I asked.

"I am going to be a father?!" He paced around as he repeated it to himself over and over again, trying to make sense of it. I walked over to him and held his hands in mine, stopping him from pacing like a crazy person.

"You will be the best one, I know it," I smiled.

"Are you so sure about that?" he asked. I could feel his clammy hands as they shook. He was nervous, and it seemed being a father scared him far more than being a chief had.

"Yes, of course I am!" I shouted.

"What should we name him?" he asked.

"How are you so sure it will be a him?"

"I don't know, just a guess." He let go of my hands and kneeled down, pressing a hand to my stomach.

"We shall see," I smiled.

"Etu...he or she will be named Etu for the sun. And if we ever have another boy, we will name him Calian after warrior of life." He looked at the deer and smiled at me.

"You're getting ahead of yourself, Catori! We still have to tell the others!" I practically jumped up and down where I stood.

"Careful!" Catori warned, taking my hand to help walk me back to the longhouse.

"If we were so careful, we wouldn't have this good news to give to everyone, would we?" I asked, smiling.

"Well said," he replied.

Epilogue

The Paugussett Tribe lived on the shoreline of what is now known as Connecticut. Their land extended from New Haven down to the Westport area. This tribe flourished on the availability of fish, shellfish, and wildlife from the coast. Due to low tide, more food such as crabs and clams would be uncovered and help them survive through the difficult winters. The springs and water were especially sacred to this tribe, as it meant life everlasting. As the Europeans came into their territory in the 17th century, deadly diseases such as smallpox were transmitted to them. At first, the Europeans worked with the Paugussett tribe for trade as they used their wampum to purchase fur from Albany, New York. The Paugussett Tribe was peaceful in the way that they tried to coexist with the Europeans, all while maintaining their rituals and customs. Unfortunately, the Europeans eventually took their land and forced what remained of the Paugussetts into starvation or freedom by running away. Some reservations were set up in the past, but additional land was continuously taken from them until none remained. Forced into assimilation, the Native Americans were able to become American citizens in the 1900s and eventually were allowed to automatically gain citizenship through birth in America.

For more information about the Paugussett Tribe, please read:

"A History of Connecticut's Golden Hill Paugussett Tribe"
by Charles Brilvitch

Charles Island Disclosure

Charles Island is located in Milford, Connecticut, and is a state park. The sandbar (tombolo) between Silver Sands State Park and Charles Island over washes twice daily with tidal flooding, which produces dangerous currents and undertow. No one should walk on any portion of the tombolo when it is covered with water.

Attention Hikers!

It is important to know walking all the way to Charles Island is not always possible. Low tides do not always uncover the tombolo completely. See Milford Harbor/Connecticut tide chart for tide details.

NO CROSSING May 1st to September 9th due to natural area preserve for nesting birds!

Acknowledgements

Thank you, Charles Brilvitch and the Bridgeport Public Library, for supplying me with a plethora of information to describe The Paugussett Tribe's customs and ways of living.

I am grateful for the Maryland Writing Association for providing countless workshops and networking opportunities to learn more about publishing and writing.

Finally, thank you to my family and friends for supporting me on my writing journey and always cheering me on and providing feedback. I couldn't do it without you!

Turn the page for a sneak peek of
Captain Kidd's curse in another Tale
of Charles Island:

AVAILABLE NOW

The Dream

1

Steady seas made for the perfect day of sailing. Persistent swishing of the waves as they gently came in against the sandy shores carried multiple shells back to sea with them again and again. When the sun peeked out of the puffy white clouds, it urged me all the more to be out there. I longed to be with the shipmates, even starting out as I did one of the worst crew-mate jobs of scrubbing the deck floors or cooking for hours on end. I could hear the floorboards creak as I walked down the deck, introducing myself to the captain, who would likely care less. Seagulls swarming the skies, letting out a screech for their own friend had taken their catch of the day. This reminded me much of humans, for many would take credit for the other's work or steal their earnings and keep them as their own. This was all a dream of mine, though. I would find myself up on this hill, peering out at the ships, thinking of how different my life would be if I had the life of a crewmate. But that was just the first step. My desire to someday be captain was the true endpoint I aimed for most. There was something about letting the wind guide your sail to and fro. A natural sense of curiosity came just from the very idea of one day having a ship of my own. A crew of my own. To voyage anywhere I wanted at any given time and have that freedom.

Each and every day, I would wake up and sneak out of my house to run up the hill to watch the sunrise. Smooth blurs of orange crept over the horizons, illuminating it in an ethereal glow, as if the very edge of earth was on fire. Instead, everything in the glow's path radiated in warmth and light. In the small town of Greenock, a picturesque landscape of mountains and valleys made up the surrounding territories aside from the lone village. Port Glasgow thrived with imports and exports—colossal ships came and went each and every day. It seemed that everyone was in a constant state of bustling around every which way. Even from the roads, you could see the ships' masts poking over roofs of houses along the way. As I climbed up the small hill near my home to watch that sunrise, I remember watching the ships in awe and utter admiration for its crew. As soon as the sun came into full view from the horizons, I jumbled back down the hill to get home before it was noticed that I snuck out. Peering down the roads, I could see Father in the top floor's window, extending both his arms up and out for a nice morning stretch. At that point, I stopped—backing up against the cold, brick wall that belonged to a building adjacent, as to not be caught out.

Peering around the corner of where I had just stood, I saw Father was no longer in the window and I ran toward the back of the house as fast as I could. That gave me just a few moments before he would be downstairs and looking for me. Beside our house, our neighbors always kept various types of flowers. Tall stalks of thistle shot out from the ground and leaned towards the sun that had just made its appearance in the sky. Contrasting with the towering stalks were delicate bluebells, which were also purple despite their name, but delicately poked out of the dew-covered grasses. Mother resembled the bluebells most. She would wake every morning before father and scurry downstairs to set a proper table with the meager portions of food that we were able to afford as a family. I did not resemble her in the slightest if not for the light green eyes that she passed down to me. I grabbed a bunch of bluebells and headed up the back steps. Mother was in on my secret as long as I didn't get caught from Father. I tried my best to sneak inside through the back door, but the creaking steps announced my presence. Before I could grasp the handle of the door in my fingers, it swung open and Father stood in the doorway, eyebrows furrowed down.

"Boy, you must not venture out there without us knowing. We've told you time and time again," I looked over at mother and saw her sympathetic face as she too must have had a dream similar to mine. But the difference with me, was that I was not going to let anything come in the way of that dream. Father must have noticed my gaze as I looked over at her instead of him and he, too, looked back at Mother who broke her eye contact with me and continued cleaning after breakfast.

"Don't think she's going to help you. If you're going to be the man of this family, you've got to straighten up," he said rigidly.

The man of the family. What a joke. That didn't seem to work very well for him. He followed everything that he was supposed to do and listened to his superiors, except we still were left with scraps of food each night despite all of his struggles each day. I would be the man of the family, but I would actually come through.

About the Author

Marissa is the author of a memoir and the Tales of Charles Island series. Marissa mostly writes fictional stories and began by journaling and writing screenplays in elementary school for her peers to perform. She spends much of her time with her pets aside from traveling to new places and journaling.

Born and raised in Connecticut, she holds New England close to her heart, and many of her stories are based in the suburbs of Connecticut.

She has a deep and profound respect for people with special needs, as her first job in her field was as a special educator. Marissa found her voice through writing. While in high school, she was the editor of the Arts and Entertainment section of the school newspaper. She pursued a degree in Education, minoring in English literature and Anthropology. Later, she went back to school to better understand Autism and graduated with a Master's in Special Education.

Marissa would love to hear from you. Use the links below to connect & hear about upcoming books:

Visit Marissa's Website:
https://www.mystywrites.com/

Instagram:
https://www.instagram.com/_mysty_writes/